ALEX SINCLAIR

THE DAY I LOST YOU

bookouture

Published by Bookouture in 2018

An imprint of StoryFire Ltd.

Carmelite House
50 Victoria Embankment
London EC4Y 0DZ

www.bookouture.com

ISBN: 978-1-78681-437-1
eBook ISBN: 978-1-78681-436-4

To my wife and daughter
Thank you for your support and inspiration

THE DAY
I LOST
YOU

ALSO BY ALEX SINCLAIR
The Last Thing I Saw

CHAPTER 1

The shadow of the apartment complex looms overhead as we make our approach to the one building in the world I despise more than any other.

"Come on, Alice," I say as we cross the wide city street, while the pedestrian light blinks at us to hurry. "We're running late enough as it is." We had to take several buses to get within walking distance of the building. Finally, we're here.

"Slow down, Mommy," Alice says as I tug her along by the hand, faster than her four-year-old legs can pump.

"I'm sorry, but we need to hurry." I hate to rush her like this, but I need to get today over with as soon as possible.

"But, Mommy, I'm tired."

"We're almost there, Bunny."

My daughter is obsessed with *Alice's Adventures in Wonderland*. No doubt because of her name and the fact I've called her Bunny ever since she was only a few days old. The White Rabbit is her favorite character. She is too young to read the book on her own, so I read it to her every night. A well-loved copy of the hardcover sits in the little backpack she's wearing.

We take the sidewalk toward the canopied entrance of the building. The metallic facade of the lobby blends seamlessly into the brick and stone complex, only adding more colorless gloom to the emerging rain clouds overhead. The combination makes the structure feel like a soul-sucking vacuum, built to draw in those with more money than sense. Like my ex-husband.

A shudder runs down my spine as we reach the entrance, almost turning me around and away. I push my irrational thoughts aside as best I can and move for the oversize handle. It's the perfect time for my anxiety to kick in.

"Mommy?" Alice asks, in her sweet, innocent voice. Her question brings me back from the brink and allows me to grip her hand once again.

"I'm okay," I tell her with a weak smile. This isn't the first time my daughter has had to witness this behavior from me, and I know it won't be the last. I try my hardest to hide it from her, but children have a way of knowing that something isn't quite right without ever needing to say so.

Alice scrunches her brow at me, unconvinced I'm okay and in control. She resists a little when I tug her along to go inside the building.

"Let's get a wriggle on, Bunny. We just have to get permission to go inside and ask to use the elevator. Then we'll take a quick ride up to the top to get your dolly back."

Alice pulls back at the prospect of riding the elevator. Ever since she was born, my little one has always feared the damn things. I wish I understood what caused her fear to develop, but unfortunately, I have no clue.

"Please, Mommy. Can we take the stairs?"

I think about her question, though I knew she was going to ask it. Typically, it wouldn't be a problem. I don't try and force Alice to face her fears. We generally take the stairs wherever we go, but we're short on time today, with fourteen floors to climb, and I have a splitting headache. We don't really have a choice, do we?

"I'll think about it, okay?" I'm rewarded with a huge grin. I'll probably cave, as usual, when the time comes; her smile could convince me to do anything.

Alice stops fighting my grip and allows me to reach for the door handle again. I see my reflection on the glass surface of the doors, as clear as day. I didn't put enough makeup on, and my dark brown hair has become frazzled in the breeze. I tried my best to straighten it in a rush this morning, but I slept through my alarm again. My eyes have bags under them that no amount of cheap makeup can conceal. Only my lipstick has managed to add any polish to my appearance.

I open up the heavy door only to see a secondary entrance ahead, with an intercom off to the side. The receptionist inside, smartly dressed in a suit and tie, has to unlock the door before we can come into the building. The setup is a new addition to the apartment complex, where I used to live. I can't even contemplate the amount of money the tenants now pay for this kind of security.

I wave to the receptionist to grab his attention. He barely looks up from the smartphone in his hand to acknowledge our existence and takes his time to buzz open the door.

We approach a central desk, placed between two support columns. The counter is three times the size it needs to be. The uninterested receptionist is still tapping away on his smartphone. I've never seen him on duty before. He doesn't appear to be a day older than twenty-five, with a clean-cut look that matches the front of the building.

"Yes?" he says with a huff as he places the phone down on the desk, but not out of sight. His gruffness catches me off guard for a moment. I consider giving him a piece of my mind, but I don't want today's trip to take a moment longer than it needs to. I study the man's nameplate and see his name is Henry.

"I'm here to see Michael Walls. He lives in one of the top-floor apartments: 1402," I say.

Henry stares at me for a moment and turns to a computer monitor at his side. He keeps his eyes level as he types the name into the system. Something comes up on his screen to prompt him to glance back to me. "And you are?"

"Erika Rice," I say, quieter than I'd like to.

This makes the guy shake his head at me slightly as another sigh escapes his lips. His phone vibrates on the counter, drawing his gaze. Without a care in the world, he reads the notification that is begging for his attention and chuckles to himself.

"Excuse me," I say. "I'm in a bit of a hurry here."

Henry's smile fades as he returns to his job. "And how do you know Mr. Walls?" he asks.

I look up at the intricate architecture of the lobby and fight back the urge to lose it. This young idiot is terrible at his job, but I shouldn't let his question get to me.

"I'm his ex-wife."

Henry responds with a raised brow before he resumes typing into his computer. I'm somewhat concerned for a moment. Has Michael not listed me in the system? It's been a while since my last visit directly to his apartment, after the unpleasantness of our failed marriage. Maybe he hasn't updated his file.

Henry studies the screen and leans closer to it; his furrowed brows put me on edge. What's written in there that is making this take so long?

"Okay, I've found you on his list of contacts as Erika Walls. I take it Mr. Walls hasn't updated your name in the system."

"Guess not," I mutter.

"Sorry?" he asks, clearly not hearing my utterance.

"Nothing. So can I see him?"

"Is he expecting you?" he asks.

I close my eyes for a moment as I try to find some patience. I can't help the feeling that's brewing inside. I refocus on Henry and answer him. "No, he isn't."

"I'll need to call him first then."

"Fine by me," I say. "Just tell him that Erika is here with his daughter."

Henry gives me his confused face again. I don't know what this guy's problem is. Alice starts to grow bored of the conversation and amuses herself by walking underneath the lip of the counter to touch its smooth surface. She is a master at always finding something to do.

"Not much longer," I whisper to her, as Henry calls Michael's apartment. I brush aside a stray hair that is covering her eyes. She's so cute; I can't help myself some days.

Henry hangs up the phone after a short time and returns to his screen. "He's not responding."

"Are you sure?" I ask. I know Michael is in. His schedule doesn't change. He's like a robot in that way.

Henry furrows his brows. "He didn't answer."

"Can you try again, please?"

A huff of contempt spills out of the man's lips as he picks up the phone again while averting his gaze. A long moment of silence passes until Henry places the receiver back down. "I'm afraid Mr. Walls is unavailable. You will need to come back another time."

"But..." I don't complete my thought. There's no point arguing with Henry. "Fine. We'll come back later, I guess."

"Have a nice day," he says, as he picks up his cell and resumes his texting.

I resist making a final comment and pull Alice along by her hand toward the exit. Alice stares up at me with her big, beautiful blue eyes. I don't care that she got the color from Michael. All I see is my Bunny when I look into them. The thought reminds me why we are here. Alice left a particular toy behind during a recent visit to Michael's apartment. It's one of her favorites: a small princess doll. I have to get it back, so I decide we'll head out to Central Park for a short while to kill some time and then try again later. If he doesn't come back, though, we'll have to continue on with our plans either way.

Alice tugs on my arm. "Mommy, I need to go to the toilet."

"Okay," I say, as I try to think of where to take her. I figure our best bet is to use the facilities here instead of the ones in the park. I turn around and call out to Henry. "Can we use the restroom?"

Henry scrunches up his face without looking at me before he nods. His eyes stay glued to his phone. I'd kill for his boss or someone important to stroll in here and catch him doing a terrible job.

"Why is that man so grumpy, Mommy?"

I chuckle at Alice's question. "I don't know, Bunny. Maybe he doesn't like his job very much."

Alice nods, her mouth half open. I don't know if she understands me or if she is just pretending. I can never quite tell.

"But you know what? It doesn't matter, because we're going to go to the restroom and then run out to the park for a play. And after that, we'll come back and hopefully see your daddy."

"Will Daddy have my dolly?" she asks.

"Of course he will. I'll bet he's got it out and ready for you to collect."

This brings a smile to Alice's face that damn near kills me. Michael and I aren't exactly on good speaking terms. The divorce was hard enough to deal with without the constant thought that Alice still needed to see her father once every two weeks. Today is an unscheduled visit so I can retrieve her toy. I know I should have checked with him first, but I hate talking to Michael on the phone as it is. Plus, I have a good reason to spring this whirlwind visit upon him.

Alice forgets all about the grumpy man as she giggles away to herself and swings my hand, skipping along to the restroom. Her little green and yellow backpack bounces up and down. We come close to reaching the restroom, but an opportunity presents itself that I cannot resist.

The elevator in the middle of the building opens up and some resident walks out. I stop on the spot and see Henry is busy dealing with another visitor I didn't notice arrive. I need to get Alice's doll back, and I figure knocking on Michael's door will be better than trying to call him. If he really isn't home and is not ignoring Henry, then I'll know I've done everything I can to get the toy back before we leave.

"Come on, Bunny," I say as I drag her toward the open door. Alice slows me down a few paces from the elevator, gripping my hand tighter than she has all morning.

"It's okay. We just have to go for a quick ride up the elevator to see if your daddy is home, so we can get your dolly. It'll only take a minute. You won't even notice."

Alice looks up at me with hope and says, "Why can't we take the stairs?"

"We don't have time for that, Bunny. But you know what? I'll be with you the entire time, okay?"

Alice lowers her head and leans closer to my side with her little four-year-old face. I'm almost tempted to take the stairs when I see her sweet, innocent frown, but I know the door to the stairwell needs a keycard to open it.

I pat her head and walk toward the closing doors. A tremor runs down my spine all of a sudden, as Alice tugs on my sleeve. "Mommy, the doors are closing."

I spin around and shove my arm through the doors without thinking. I feel my heart boom in my chest. I should never have done that in front of Alice, but I'm in a hurry. We walk into the elevator a moment later and settle into place, staring out into the lobby. I can't help but think about why I am so desperate to get Alice's doll back, and what I have planned. It's not going to go well. Nothing ever does.

My hands begin to shake as another hit of anxiety does its best to attack me. I try to steady myself by pressing my palms against my face so I can concentrate on my breathing, but my tactic fails to work with thoughts of Michael cramming my brain.

I slap the close-door button with one hand, frustrated that the elevator has chosen now to take forever to shut.

"Mommy?" Alice asks as the double doors seal tight. As the outside world is cut off, my daughter's voice brings me back.

"Sorry, Bunny. Mommy isn't feeling well today."

"Are you sick?" Alice asks with a curious voice. She's trying to make sense of why I am the way I am, and I hate that I can't explain it to her. I wish I could hide it better, so she didn't have to feel even a second of worry.

"No. Mommy just needs a moment to relax a little. Now, enough silly business. We need to travel up, so we can go see your daddy and get your dolly back. Just a quick ride and we're there."

"Yeah, Daddy!" Alice's eyes light up again at the mention of her father—not so much for her dolly. It pains me to see that face, but I tell myself that this visit is to get her toy back. She's going to need it over the next few weeks.

After a few short breaths in and out, I fumble with the level-fourteen button. The jolt of the motor kicks into action. Alice grips on tight and lets out a tiny squeak as we head up to the top floor. I should be reassuring her that everything will be okay, that we'll be seeing her father in no time, but I can't stop thinking about what I'm going to say if he is home. Will he know what I'm up to?

Alice wraps herself around my body as we ascend at a rapid pace. I refocus on the task at hand and try to push out my twisted thoughts. The visit is going to be hard enough without any distractions, because little does Michael know that I am here to get Alice's doll back and leave with Alice forever. If he is home, he is about to see his daughter for the last time.

CHAPTER 2

Then

I couldn't wait for Michael to get home to our tiny one-bedroom apartment in Brooklyn. He had no idea that I had taken the day off sick, using the free time to do something I'd been dying to do for two years. I'd gotten home from the doctor's office after a two-hour wait, with a blood test confirming I was pregnant.

For the last two years, we'd been trying to conceive a child. Michael and I were determined to have a baby and start the family we both craved. After being married for six years, through all of the good and the bad, we'd reached that point where we both wanted to take our relationship to the next level. The decision felt right.

But want and reality were two different things. Like every person before us that had decided to have a go at becoming a parent, we thought conceiving a baby would be a breeze. At most, we thought we'd have to wait three months before I'd get the positive test result. When five months had gone by, I started to doubt our ability to fall pregnant.

"It's never going to happen," I'd say to Michael. He'd shrug me off with a smile and tell me not to worry. Maybe I was in a rush, but my intentions were pure. I just wanted to hold a little person in my hands who looked like the perfect blend of Michael and me.

The next thing we knew, it had been a year. Twelve months of failed tests and crushed hopes. Nothing either of us said or thought could change the fact that something was up. We had sex like clockwork at the right times, yet still I could not get a positive test result.

Michael was thirty. I was three months out from my twenty-ninth birthday. We had no medical history that would suggest there was a problem, but something was causing a delay.

"What if this never happens? What if we can't have a baby? Will you still love me?" I'd ask.

"It'll happen," Michael said. "And of course I'd still love you. I'd love you no matter what happened. We simply have to keep trying. That's what the doctor said." We'd just come back from getting fertility tests done. The results showed no issues with either of us. We were told in a dismissive tone merely to keep at it until we got a positive test.

"But what if it doesn't happen?" I asked him over and over. He'd tell me what I needed to hear, reassuring me it was nobody's fault. But another month would go by without anything happening. The pressure was beginning to take its toll on my hopes.

By the time we were eighteen months past the first night we had tried, Michael avoided talking about our attempts to fall pregnant. It wasn't that he didn't care; he was merely trying to spare my feelings.

With our attempts to have a baby out of the spotlight, Michael started spending more time working after hours on his résumé, doing everything possible to get a foot in the door at a bigger law firm. After some time all he ever talked about was his attempts to get a job at a big firm, where the "real money" was.

When we were one month out from the two-year mark, I almost gave up on the idea that we'd ever have a baby. I spent the next thirty days getting used to the fact that it would never happen and tried to think what I would focus all of my energy on instead.

So that morning, when I got a positive result, I could barely believe it. I took another test. Three positive sticks later, I called into work for a full day off, so I could go to the doctor's and confirm everything with a blood test. None of it felt real until the doctor confirmed what the tests had already told me. I felt weightless, looking forward to the wonderful surprise I'd get to give Michael. It had finally happened! I let a sense of relief wash over me; I could now go to my husband and give him the news we'd wanted to hear for so long.

I left everything out on the counter for Michael to see, as I waited patiently for him to arrive. He would be home any minute. When he discovered that I was pregnant, he would see that there was still hope for us, that we could be a family. I'd make him see that there were more rewarding things in the world than a career, and that I could be a good mother.

The door to the apartment unlocked with a click as Michael twisted his keys and jiggled the lock. He pushed the door open and shuffled inside, briefcase and coat in hand. His tie was already undone, his collar unbuttoned. He had killed himself again, trying to climb the ladder. My news would show him that he didn't need to do that anymore. We could focus on our child instead.

"Hi, honey," he called out when he saw me. He dumped his gear down and ran a hand through his tousled hair.

"Hello," I said, as I stepped over to him, trying to contain the smile dying to burst out of me. "How was your day?" I leaned up and kissed him on the cheek. His tired face edged into a smile.

"Good to see you too, honey," he said. "You're never going to believe what happened at work today."

I glanced back to the counter to the blood test. I couldn't wait. He had to know. "Can I show you something first?"

"Just a sec. I've got something important to tell you." He drew me in with both hands on my shoulders. I gazed into his eyes, trying to predict what he was about to tell me. It was something big, I knew that much.

"I got the job," he whispered.

"Sorry?" I asked, as if I didn't understand English.

"I got the job," he repeated, with a lot more vigor. "You are now looking at the newest lawyer to join the team at Morris & Wilcox."

"Oh my god, honey. That's amazing," I said, almost stunned to hear his news. I twisted back to the counter. My big news would have to wait a moment.

"You're damn right it is. We're talking triple the salary for the same number of hours. Things are going to change, so much. We can finally afford to move out of this damn shoebox apartment into a real place with a few spare bedrooms."

I faced him again with a smile at the thought of those spare bedrooms and gave him a hug. I spoke over his shoulder as we embraced. "I'm so proud of you, honey. You got the job! I can't believe it."

"Thank you. I was beginning to doubt myself for a minute there, but I knew if I just kept persisting, they'd take me on. Damn, it feels good."

"I'll bet," I said, as Michael moved further into the apartment. He went past the test results on the kitchen counter, straight to the fridge. He pulled out two beers and twisted them open. He handed me a bottle and clinked his against mine with a "Cheers" before taking a big swig. I stood there and watched as he swallowed a third of the liquid in one gulp.

He stood there, one hand on the counter, the other lifting his beer for another swig. He glanced over to me once he had finished smiling to himself. "You gonna drink that or what?" He knew I should have been on my period by now. I'd thought I was just a little late—my scheduled test had come back negative. But a few days later, I was still late, so I'd tried another test this morning.

"I can't," I said.

"What do you mean you can't? It's a beer. I've seen you drink them plenty of times before."

"Okay then, I'm not allowed to."

Michael stared at me with a confused frown. He still wasn't getting it.

"Wait. If it's because you want to drink the good stuff to celebrate, I understand. The beer is just a placeholder. You and I are going to hit the town tonight and do this right."

"That's not it, honey," I said, my voice slightly above a whisper. "Why don't you take a look at those pieces of paper sitting there."

Michael leaned sideways a little. "What is this?" he asked as he picked up the medical note. His eyes darted left and right as he absorbed the information. "Wait. Is this saying…?"

"Yes," I said, as I leaped toward him. "We're pregnant. It finally happened." I was right in front of him, gazing into his eyes to see his reaction. His mouth hung open. A smile slowly stretched out across his face.

"Is this for real?" he asked with a chuckle.

"It is, honey. We did it."

"We did it," he echoed. "It finally happened. We're having a baby."

My mind was filled with a thousand different things at once. All of it good, for a change. To see Michael smile with happiness that could not be matched by anything else was beyond amazing. I had stupid fears that he would leave me for someone who could give him a child. Especially considering the amazing opportunity he had just received.

I shoved my doubts away and focused on our celebration. We hugged for a long while. Michael kept muttering in my ear: "I can't believe it. This is crazy. First I get the job, now this."

I pulled back. "You're happy about this, right?"

"Yes. More than anything else in the world. I just can't believe how lucky I am right now."

"We deserve this," I said. "It's been two long years. Finally, we're getting rewarded for our hard work."

"We are," he said. "This is our time. Things are going to be perfect."

That was almost five years ago. Our future seemed bright. The possibilities felt endless. Little did I know that our marriage was on a downward spiral I could never stop.

CHAPTER 3

Now

The ride up seems to be taking longer than it should. The elevator in this building is supposed to be an express system when you select the top floor. I'm on edge straight away that the elevator is taking so long to reach its destination.

"Mommy? Why does Daddy live on the top floor?"

I sigh and put on a happy face to answer Alice. I must respond to questions like this thirty times per day. She's at that curious age; she wants an answer to her every thought.

"Well, Bunny, your daddy has a very important job for a company that pays him a lot of money. That means he can afford to live at the top of a building like this."

"Okay," Alice says with a twisted brow. I doubt she fully understands me, but how else can I explain it?

Michael sends me child support and pays my rent every month. He's never been late with a single payment and makes sure I know it. I refuse to take alimony on top of that, not wanting a cent more of his precious money than is needed to give Alice the life she deserves. I would rather work my low-paying admin job and earn the money I need than give him the satisfaction of paying my way in full.

His career was part of the reason we split up, when Alice was only six months old. His beloved job at the law firm always came first. Alice came second; he'd spend time with her after a long day at work. I was continuously the last thing he thought about. I was lucky if he said two words to me per day.

What initiated our relationship's descent was something I couldn't stop from happening. I never imagined things would go that way in a million years, yet he blamed me for that day and refused to forgive me for it.

The elevator comes to a sudden stop. I stumble a little as it shakes with a jolt. Alice grips my clothing and legs tighter than before. Then, all we hear is silence. The motors aren't grinding away to defy gravity and haul us up to the top of the building. There is no electrical hum. Just a creaking groan from above that sends a stab of panic straight down into my body.

"Mommy?" Alice asks. I should have spoken first to reassure her everything is fine, but my mouth doesn't want to function. My fear matches hers.

She tugs at my leg. I stare down to see her eyes well up. "It's okay, Bunny. The elevator has stopped. Nothing to worry about." I squat down to her level and run my hand gently over her cheek. I pull her in tight before the tears truly begin to flow.

"Mommy will check it and see what's going on. Just stand here by the wall and hold on to the rail." I guide Alice over and place her hand up to the metal bar. I turn around to the panel and take in a deep breath as the overhead lights flicker off and back on. We must be stuck just before level seven, based on the readout.

"God," I mutter to myself. Of all the days for the elevator system to screw up, it had to be when we were coming to see Michael unscheduled. I shake my head and try to focus on the task at hand, instead of trying to find every negative thing about the current situation. It's a coping strategy recommended to me by my doctor. I have no idea if it really works or not.

"Okay," I say to myself. Apart from the floor numbers, there are few options to press other than door open, door close, and emergency stop. There is an emergency call button, but I don't want to press that until I have to. Henry will have me thrown out of the building if we have to call anyone for help. I know we didn't touch the stop button or any others by accident. We were both huddled in the middle, waiting out the long ride up to the top.

I slap the number fourteen a few times to see if I can get things going. Nothing happens. "What the heck?" I say, watching my language. I try again and get the same result.

"What's wrong, Mommy?" Alice calls out behind me.

I turn back to her just as the lights all go out and throw the elevator into complete darkness. I hear her breath quicken as panic sets in. It takes everything I have not to fall victim to the same fear. I close my eyes and try not to imagine the elevator plummeting down the shaft.

"Bunny, it's okay. The lights went out. Come to my voice." I reach out my hands, trying to find her in the dark. Why can't I find her? She should be close by. I step forward until I reach the metal wall of the elevator. "What?" I mutter, realizing I must have stumbled in the wrong direction. "Bunny? Alice?" She should be answering me.

I realize I can't hear her breathing. Has she fallen over? Has she squashed herself down to the floor to hide from the dark? I decide enough is enough, and claw through my bag to find my cell and activate its obscenely bright flashlight. I unlock the screen and fire up the light. My eyes take a second to adjust as the brightness reflects off every metallic surface inside the car. Alice is not where I left her. My heart skips a beat.

"Mommy?" she says from behind.

I spin around and unintentionally shine the light in her eyes. "Thank God," I say. My shoulders relax from their tense state. Alice is now by the control panel. We must have gone right by each other in the dark. How could I be so stupid to not notice her like that?

"Stay there, Bunny. I'm going to try and call someone." I bring my phone up to my face, leaving the flashlight on, as I try to work out who I can even call.

"But, Mommy, there are lights over here." Alice starts pressing buttons before I can get a word out.

"No, Bunny, don't do—"

The elevator doors pop open with a ding, but stop after only a single foot. That's when I get confirmation that we are not quite at the seventh level. The car's floor hasn't quite matched up with seven's landing, and there is a small step up to it through the narrow gap.

Alice charges to the light pouring into the elevator from the seventh floor.

"Bunny, wait. That door could close on us at any moment."

Alice stops in front of the opening and stares out to the floor. She doesn't say a word.

"Come back to Mommy," I say. I try not to let the thought of her getting crushed by closing doors pin me down with fear.

"But I don't like it in here. It's dark and scary. I want to take the stairs."

"It's okay, Bunny. I'm here for you. I'll keep us safe." I try to move toward her, but my legs feel too heavy.

Alice shakes her head and steps further into the gap.

"What are you doing?" I yell. I fight through the feeling of being rooted to the ground and rush toward my daughter as she climbs through the space and up into the seventh floor.

"Alice, come back here right now," I say as she runs away. I find myself wedged in the door as I try to push through.

"I'm going to find Daddy," Alice says. "He'll know what to do."

"No, Bunny," I yell. "He's not on this floor. Alice, come back here."

It's the worst time for the elevator to start shaking, and then it drops almost a foot down. My phone falls out onto the seventh floor with a sickening thud and slides away. My heart skips a beat and then pumps with fear as a vision of being crushed to death fills my mind. The sudden jolt of the elevator scares Alice further away from me, and she stumbles backward.

Then, without warning, the doors begin to squeeze shut. I'm still too deep in the elevator to push my way out. The car drops again, this time only a small amount, but the doors continue to squeeze closed around me. I realize I have no other option but to fall back inside.

I focus on Alice with wide eyes. "Stay there, Bunny. Don't go anywhere. Mommy will come find you once she gets this door open, I promise."

"Okay, Mommy," she says to me as I squeeze backward and watch the elevator doors seal shut. The lights flick back on along with the sound of the motor.

The display flashes at me with its next intended target. That's when I realize I'm heading back down to the lobby, while Alice is stuck on the seventh floor—alone.

CHAPTER 4

The elevator plummets back down as I watch each floor tick by on the display above me. The car seems to be taking forever to reach the lobby as I pace around in a panicked rush.

"Come on, come on," I mutter to myself.

I stand at the front while the elevator settles slowly to the ground floor. The doors pop open with a ping, and I see a few people waiting.

"I need to go back up. My daughter is stuck on the seventh floor," I yell as I slap the button to close the doors. For some reason, they remain defiantly open. A few crooked glances come my way, along with some muted comments as the confused group exchange complaints.

I couldn't care less if I've ruined their day; my daughter is in this oversize building alone. I slap the seventh-floor button over and over. Nothing happens.

"Come on," I let out as I try again to close the doors. It isn't until my third attempt at bashing the button that I realize the panel is entirely unresponsive. I try to reason why, but no rational thoughts come to mind. All I can think about is getting back to Alice.

"Are you okay, miss?" one of the people asks. "Did you say your daughter is stuck on the seventh floor?"

"Yes!" I say to the woman without looking toward her. "I need to get back up there right now."

"Okay," she replies. "Go see the young man on reception. He'll help you out."

"No, no, no," is all I can say as I try to fix the problem myself by slapping my palm against every button. No amount of frustration will repair it.

I pace around in a circle as I try to find a solution. I shake out my hands, flopping my wrists hard. Nothing comes to mind. I'm going to have a panic attack any second now if I don't generate an idea. Think, dammit.

I can hear my breath tighten.

I can feel the world closing in.

I can taste blood in my mouth.

"Alice?" I ask out loud.

Running out of the elevator, I charge past the three people. I knock a man's groceries to the floor in the process as I rush back to reception, back to Henry. I ignore the complaints behind me and focus on the receptionist. I don't care that he will find out that I used the elevator without his permission. All that matters is finding Alice.

When I arrive at the desk, I see him still talking to the same old man from before. I interrupt a one-sided conversation about the reliability of the mail.

"Henry!" I yell.

"Just one moment," he says holding up a finger without looking back.

"No, please listen. I need help. My daughter is stuck on the seventh floor." My words grab Henry's full attention and turn him around to face me.

"Your daughter? What are you talking about?" Henry says, somewhat confused. "Wait, what were you doing on the seventh floor? I never gave you permission to—"

"Listen to me, please. My four-year-old girl is alone on the seventh floor of this building."

"I'm sorry to hear that, but you need to take a moment to calm down and—"

"Don't tell me to calm down! My little girl is missing. She's up there all alone and lost. I need to get into the stairwell." I don't care that I'm shouting until I see at least ten people in the lobby staring in my direction. Even the three people by the elevator are still around, watching the drama unfold. Why aren't they helping me? This isn't a joke.

The old man steps toward me. His eyes seem familiar, but I can't quite place him. "Excuse me, miss, how did your little girl end up on the seventh floor alone?" he asks with a calm voice.

I flick my eyes to the man, wondering who he is. He's a short and skinny senior with thinning hair.

"The damn elevator got stuck there and partially opened. My Bunny can't stand elevators and freaked out. She escaped through the gap just before the doors shut and sent me back down to the ground."

The old man tilts his head slightly at me. "Did you say 'Bunny'?"

I close my eyes tight and frown while both of my hands grip my skull. "I meant Alice. Bunny is her nickname."

"It's a cute name. I like it," he says, as I open my eyes again. "Don't worry. We'll find little Bunny soon enough." He walks over from the front of the reception desk and offers me his hand to shake. "My name is Alan Bracero. I'm a resident of Stonework Village. Now, I can personally guarantee that your daughter will be fine. There's not much up on seven. Most of the apartments aren't being rented out at the moment. Why were you heading there, anyway?"

"I wasn't," I say, thankful that he seems to know so much about the building. "I was going to the top floor."

Alan's brows twist. "Then why did your daughter get off at seven?"

"I told you—the elevator got stuck, and the doors opened enough for her to slip through. She hates elevators. They scare her. I should have gotten access to the stairs. God, I'm an awful mother."

Alan shakes his head. "Now, now. Calm yourself, miss. I'm sorry, but what you're saying doesn't make sense. If you were heading up to fourteen, you shouldn't have stopped at seven."

I step back a pace as I resist the urge to freak out. I know Alan is trying to help quiet me down, but my Bunny is up there all alone. I see her confused face in my mind. I can't help my reaction.

"Listen to me when I say this: the elevator screwed up and got stuck at seven." I step closer to Alan and stare into his eyes while breathing audibly. The next words out of my mouth are as calm as I can make them. "Then, the doors opened, and my daughter escaped. The elevator closed and took me back down here, and now it won't work."

"Just take it easy," Henry says, butting in with two raised palms like I'm about to explode. "We'll find Alice, but first you need to take a moment and simmer down."

"Simmer down? My baby girl is on her own in a fourteen-level building, and you want me to take it easy? I need to get up there right now."

I ignore the eyes of those around me as the world closes in like I'm a danger. Do none of these people have children? Can they honestly tell me they wouldn't behave the same way?

"I'll assist you, ma'am," Alan says.

"Thank you," I reply, not waiting to hear what Henry has to say on the issue.

Alan moves toward the elevator at a pace that surprises me. He seems rather active for his age. I catch up to his side with a few hasty steps.

"I'm the head of the neighborhood watch for the building," he says, as he waves off the three people about to board the elevator. I feel a slight sense of relief—something is finally being done. I'll see Alice soon enough. I rub the back of my wrists as I feel my heart thumping away.

The double doors to the elevator have managed to close at some point during my yelling. I start shuffling on the spot as we wait. Alan presses the button a few times before stepping closer to me.

"Wait. I can't take the elevator again. This thing is taking too long to open. It screwed up before and it'll screw up again. I don't think it's even working. We're taking the stairs."

"Nonsense. This will be much quicker."

"I know it will, but I'm not doing it," I say, as I head to the stairs. Alan follows. I'm not going to get on that thing again and get stuck somewhere else while my Bunny needs me.

"Are you going to help me or not?"

Alan purses his lips with a lowered head. "I will. We'll take the stairs, but I have to say that your way is going to take a lot longer."

"I understand, but it's safer."

He throws his hands up in defeat. "Okay. Do you know about the keycard system?"

"Yes. I used to live here," I say.

I don't waste another moment and rush over to the stairwell door. Alan swipes his keycard over the panel to unlock the entrance. I push through first. A second later I am climbing up the building, with Alan right on my tail, to find my little Bunny.

CHAPTER 5

Alan keeps up with me as we hurry upward. The stairwell is made from solid concrete, meaning we have no way of seeing up or down. Not being able to see ahead adds another rock to my stomach. We maintain a silence that is deafening until Alan speaks.

"What's your name, dear? You look so damn familiar."

"Erika. I lived in the building for a short amount of time."

He grunts. "Right. Maybe I've seen you around here."

"I doubt it," I mutter.

"Well then, if we haven't met before, I'm pleased to meet you, Erika. I'm sorry it's under such terrible circumstances."

"Same to you, Alan," I say, attempting to be polite after realizing I've no doubt been rude to everyone who's crossed my path since Alice fled the elevator. "I'm sorry for getting upset with you before. I'm just a bit anxious to find Alice."

"I understand. I have a few kids of my own. Of course, they're all grown up now. You said your daughter is four years old?"

"Yes."

Alan smiles at me. "Fun age, that one."

"Yes, it is. All the more reason why I'm so desperate to find her."

"Uh, yes, I understand," Alan replies. He clears his throat. "So why were you headed to the top floor, if you don't mind me asking?"

I sigh. Why does he want to know? "I was taking Alice up there to see if her father, Michael Walls, was home. He's a lawyer who lives in one of the top-floor apartments."

Alan's brows lift at the mention that my ex is a lawyer. He might know who Michael is from his neighborhood watch, but he doesn't know what kind of relationship Michael and I have, apart from the fact that I don't live here. Hopefully, the knowledge that Alice's father is a lawyer will be enough to scare him into taking this a little more seriously.

"I see," Alan says. "Well, best we find your little one then."

"Yes. That's all I want."

By this point, Alice must be so scared. No one is there to tell her everything is okay. No one is there to calm her down and hold back her tears. I know what people are like; none of them will come out from their apartments to help a lost child.

My little Bunny escaped that elevator out of fear; whatever reason she has to be afraid of elevators will be permanent after today. I'll never make her ride another one again.

Alan continues talking to me, possibly trying to keep me distracted. Finally, we reach the entry to the seventh floor and pull the door inward to open it.

"Bunny," I call out, as I step into the carpeted corridor. The stairs come out next to the elevator in the middle of the building's H shape. I take a quick peek left and right. I feel the hairs on my body stand on their ends when I don't immediately spot her. Why isn't she near?

Light fixtures above dot the way. I compose myself and find the courage to continue. I have to be strong for her. "Alice, where are you? Mommy's here." My voice disappears down the long corridors. I spin left and then right, looking in the two directions she could have run off. The doors had shut on me too quickly: I didn't get a chance to see which route she chose.

"Alice?" Alan calls out. "Come on out."

I shake my head at the old man. "She won't come to the sound of a stranger's voice. I taught her not to. Please, let me call out to her." I turn away as Alan nods his head to show he understands.

I try my hardest not to sound ungrateful, but it's hard not to. I just want to find Alice before the situation gets out of hand and before Michael finds out. I know he would try to use this against me. He's always trying to prove how bad a mother I am.

"Bunny," I shout down the left corridor before pacing over to the right and doing the same on the other side of the H-shaped layout.

"If I may interrupt?" Alan says.

I half face him, still glancing all around, in search mode. "Yes?"

"May I suggest we split up? I know your little girl will probably run in the opposite direction if she sees an old fool like me, but I can call out to you the second I find her."

I close my eyes for a moment to center my thoughts. "Okay. That sounds like a good idea."

Alan gives me a quick nod. "I'll head left. You take the right."

"Thank you," I say, as I watch him go left. That's when I remember losing my phone near the elevator. I quickly scan the area and discover it's nowhere to be found. Did Alice pick it up? I hope she did. Or maybe one of the residents found it? It doesn't matter now. I can always replace it with a new one.

I rush off in the opposite direction as the overhead lights buzz. I continue to call out to Alice, alternating between her nickname and her actual name. Every time I shout out, my voice bounces down the corridor, diminishing as it reverberates off the walls and the closed doors.

The passageway is littered with apartment entrances. I want to bang on each door I find and ask the occupants if they have seen a little girl, but I resist for now. I first need to sweep the floor before I start to panic in full. It's not far off at this point.

Once I reach the end of the corridor, I find two options again that she could have taken. Left or right. I head right. The floor is crammed full of apartments. Alan said that most of the units on this level are empty, meaning we won't have many people to help find Alice if needed. The place feels devoid of life.

What should have been a thriving residential floor full of people who could have helped find Alice is instead a maze of nothing. There aren't many places a small child could hide, unless they found their way into an empty, unlocked apartment.

I call out to Alice again. I hate the sound of my voice weakening against the concrete walls. Where the hell is she? "Bunny!" I shout as my pace quickens. "Alice, please come out. Mommy's here."

I reach the end of the right side and turn around to cover the opposite section to the left past the middle corridor. There are dozens of apartments along this section of the building. Could she have gone inside one of them? I reach the other end.

Nothing.

I charge back the way I came, shouting her name while checking every nook and cranny. I again pass the central row that holds the elevator and stairwell. A sting of sweat prickles my forehead. Why can't I find her?

Finally, I feel it hit me square in the face: panic. I gulp in rapid breaths of air and start to spin around in the long corridor. I can't fight this anymore. I turn and turn, my hands shaking. I try desperately to pull my palms to my face, but I stumble and drop into a squat on the thick carpet before I can center myself. All I see is Alice, terrified and alone, as I feel myself breaking down.

After a moment of shaking, I wrap my arms around my face and begin to sense the calm flow over me. I hear my breathing slow enough to allow me to think again. Then, as if on cue, the little voice in my head starts to question me.

How could I have let this happen? I've lost my only daughter inside this damn building, while Michael possibly sits on the top floor, oblivious. Whether he's here or not doesn't matter. As soon as he finds out Alice went missing even for a second, he will happily use it against me. The only reason we were coming here today was to get Alice's toy back before we left town for good.

I'm so rattled that I doubt I'll be able to go through with the idea even if I find Alice in the next ten seconds.

"Miss?" Alan says, back from his search of the other side of the building.

I realize how strange it must look to him that I am squatting down with both arms covering my face. I fight through the embarrassment and rise to my feet and straighten my hair.

"Is everything okay?" he asks, taking long strides in my direction.

I run toward him. "Please tell me you've seen Alice," I say in a choked voice. I already know he hasn't found her, but I need him to say it. I need to hear the words come from his mouth. I close the gap between us and grab hold of him by his jacket.

Alan shakes his head while leaning back from me. "I didn't see her, I'm afraid. I've checked my side and I can see she's not here either."

"Okay," I let out with a squeak. I let go of him and stumble back. I'm fighting back the tears as I try to speak. My words won't come. I begin to pace around while shaking out my wrists.

Alan stares at me with sympathetic eyes. I already know what he is going to tell me next, but I wait for him to say it out loud.

"She's not here."

I grab my head and squeeze. I look up to Alan and try to hold back the fear brewing inside. How long can I keep this up for? "Where is she?"

"There's only one place she could have gone," he says.

I step toward him again, my eyes wide. "Where? Tell me, please."

"Follow me." He turns and resumes his quick pace.

I charge up behind and follow. We rush back down the middle corridor toward the elevator. We arrive at the steel doors but veer off toward the stairwell access point.

"You don't think?" I ask.

"I'm guessing she went this way," Alan says.

The handle is low and within Alice's reach. She worked out how our doors at home functioned at a young age. I press on the handle; it moves with ease, and the door swings open onto the stairwell. Only the door to the lobby locks from the outside. She could have gone up or down in an attempt to find her daddy or me. If she went down, she had to have exited onto another floor, or we would have seen her. If she went up, the same possibility existed. How far could her little legs have taken her?

Alan steps through beside me. "I could head up, and you could go back down. If I find her, I'll give your cell a call. What's your number?"

Alice couldn't have gone that far up or down. I know it in my heart. She's only small. Then I remember my cell is missing. "Dammit. I lost my phone when the elevator screwed up. I thought we were going to find it out there."

Alan nods at me and looks around the area, thinking up a new idea. "Maybe Alice picked it up. We should try calling it."

I close my eyes as I struggle to remember my own phone number. I can recall maybe half of it in my head, but the rest is a scrambled mess. "I don't know it. How can I not know my own number? I'm so stupid."

"It's okay. What about Michael? He should know it, right? Why don't we give him a call and find out your number? If he's nearby, he can help with the search."

"No, we can't," I blurt. I realize a second too late that it might seem a bit odd that I don't want Alice's father to help find her as quickly as possible. I should have told Alan from the start that we don't have the best relationship.

Alan stares at me with a frown. "Why not? I'd imagine he'd be quite keen to ensure the safety of his daughter."

"He would be," I say, "but I don't want to bother him with this."

"Bother him?" Alan says, as he crosses his arms over his chest. His brow tightens. "I know you two are split up, but he would want to know Alice is okay."

I give him a slight scowl. "How did you know we weren't together?"

"Well, you don't live together, for starters. But hey, I get it. I've been there. You don't ever want them to have the upper hand, for any reason, but this is different. This is serious. I'm sure Michael would only want to see his daughter found."

I close my eyes and try to push out the image of Michael screaming at me, telling me I'm a worthless excuse for a mother. I am, though. I lost her. This is all my fault. I sigh with a heavy heart, knowing that Alan is right. There's no other option.

"Okay. Let's call him. We have to."

CHAPTER 6

Then

Pregnancy was harder than I thought it would be. I was two months along and still able to hide from my employer the fact that I had a baby growing inside me—for now. What I couldn't hide was the aggressive morning sickness that knocked me on my ass every day. All I wanted to do was vomit, but it would never happen. I'd crouch over the toilet at home or the office and try to will the contents of my stomach up to get some sense of relief, but it would never happen.

A visit to my doctor confirmed everything was fine and that this was just a frustrating, yet regular, part of the process. It didn't seem possible that such a tiny thing inside you could cause so much pain. I'd known that it was going to be tough, but I wasn't prepared for so much nausea every day. On top of that, I was exhausted. How was I going to handle this when I was six-plus months pregnant? I'd have to go to work every day until the last possible minute. Would the stress I'd feel be good for the baby?

Michael had started his new job in Manhattan and came home later and later each day. I wanted to tell him that I needed him back with me as early as possible because of my morning sickness, but he was too busy with the job he had just started. I understood he was trying to make an impression, but at the same time, I needed him more.

My desire wasn't from any demand to have my own personal servant waiting on me hand and foot. I just wanted him to hold me and make me feel better. I wanted reassurance that I wasn't just some baby machine to him, but also his wife.

It was getting later and later each day that he came home. I thought the extra hours would make him bitter and resentful of people like me who held a regular job, but he seemed to thrive on the pressure. Instead of coming home exhausted, he'd spend his night working on a case. He'd occasionally ask about the baby to ensure I was doing everything perfectly, so it grew the right way. He started to focus in on the pregnancy more than he did on me. When he texted me during the day, he began to ask more about the baby and less about how I was coping.

"Are you going to check how my day was?" I asked him. He'd finished grilling me for the night about the baby and had jumped onto his laptop.

He pointed his head in my direction, but his eyes stayed glued to the screen. "Sorry?"

He hadn't heard a word. I might as well have been talking to the thin walls of our apartment. Maybe the neighbors would care about what I had to say.

"Never mind," I said. "Just go back to your work. It's more important than me, apparently."

Michael turned to face me fully and closed the laptop. He slid the favored device away across the small dining table and cleared his throat. "It's not like that, honey. It's just that I've got an important client starting tomorrow. I'm trying to get in front of it, is all. What did you want to talk about?"

I shook my head. "It's fine. I don't want to interrupt. I just wanted to spend some time with you."

"Erika, please," he said sternly. He stood up and moved in my direction. He sat down beside me on the two-seater couch we'd managed to squeeze into the living room. "I know this has been tough on you, so I want to do something to make it all better."

"What are you talking about?" I asked, skepticism lining my thoughts.

"Your job."

"What about it?"

"How would you like to call your boss tomorrow and tell her to stick it?"

I tilted my head, trying to understand what he was talking about.

"Hear me out. I'm about to get a big bonus for one of the first clients I worked on. If it goes through okay, I think we could afford for you to quit your job."

I exhaled, not realizing I'd been holding my breath for a few seconds. It was a habit I needed to put a stop to right away. I didn't know if it harmed the baby in any way, but what was bad for me had to be bad for it. "I don't know if that's such a good idea."

"Why?" he asked.

"Well, what if you lost your job?"

Michael chuckled. "Trust me, that's not going to happen. They love me. I can see them offering me partner one day."

"How can you be so sure? It's only been two months."

He nodded away with raised brows. "I see where you're coming from, but two months is a long time. Enough for a person to establish they are a team player, willing to do what it takes to win for their firm."

My head lowered with his words. I could hear in his voice how much he valued this new life of his. I could detect how much he wanted to be the breadwinner for his family. I could tell he was thinking this way more and more as time went on. On the one hand, it was sweet of him to want to take on the burden, but at the same time it would mean more time at the office.

"You want me to quit my job. Why?"

"So you can take it easy at home and avoid the frustrations of the city. Maybe if you weren't so stressed out with work, the morning sickness wouldn't be such a big deal."

"A big deal? Are you complaining about it?"

"No, not like that. I mean maybe it wouldn't drain you so much if you could go rest for a few hours instead of resuming your duties in a stuffy office. And it would be so much better for the baby, right?"

"Okay," I said, allowing the thought to sink in. Being at home would help me with my morning sickness. "Hypothetically, what would I tell my work? I've never quit a job before."

"The truth. You're pregnant, and you need to focus on getting through that more than you need the stress of an office job."

I lowered my head in thought, trying to weigh up the pros and cons. I liked my admin job. I worked for a large company with a huge staff. I loved the people there, the work I did, and the social environment only an office job could provide. On the other hand, it would be nice not to have to deal with the commute and the politics that came with it. There were days when everyone managed to annoy me. Being heavily pregnant wouldn't make that any easier.

I glanced up into Michael's eyes and saw how badly he wanted this. I thought about the baby and the many benefits it would get if I were to throw in the towel and stay at home. I couldn't help but wonder if Michael's concern seemed to focus on our unborn child above anything—or anyone—else. But I wanted to keep him happy in any way I could. With that thought and Michael's pleading eyes, the answer was clear. I had no other choice.

"Okay, I'll do it. End of the week, I'll put in my notice. A few weeks after that, I'll be done."

"That's wonderful, honey," he said. "This will be a good thing; I promise you." He wrapped his arms around my body and held me gently. He kissed my cheek and softly rubbed the tiny baby bump that only he knew existed. Then he stood up again to move back to his seat at the small dining table in our open-plan apartment where his laptop waited. He plonked down and opened the lid again. I watched the screen come to life, revealing boring spreadsheets and documents.

I stared at Michael as he got back to work, while I tried to foolishly debate if I'd made the right choice by listening to him.

CHAPTER 7

Now

Michael doesn't answer his cell. I got the number from his business card, which I keep in my handbag, his name embossed and shiny.

I hand Alan back his cell. "He won't answer. Now what?" I ask, like he has all the solutions at his fingertips.

He scratches at his chin for a moment and comes up with an obvious idea. "We should keep searching up the stairwell. If we don't find her, then we can knock on Michael's door and see if he's home. He might be able to help us locate her."

"Okay, yes. We have to," I say, as my shoulders drop. If we don't find her by the time we reach the top floor, I don't know how I'll cope. The thought sends a shudder down my spine. Even after going through the torture of searching the stairs, I'll still have to show up at Michael's without Alice. It will kill me, if it comes to that, but I have no choice.

I start to walk for the stairs, but Alan raises his palm for me to stop.

"Better yet, why don't I take the stairs down and you take the stairs up to Michael's. At least that way we can cover the entire stairwell at the same time. I'll do a quick sweep of each floor on my way down. You just go straight up to Michael's. If you don't find her, knock on his door so he can help you search each floor back down. I'll wait in the lobby for you when I reach the bottom. Hopefully, one of us finds her."

It's a good idea. We won't be wasting any time if we split up. My only concern is if Alan does find Alice on the way down. She won't know who he is or if he can be trusted. I'll also have no way of knowing he's found her. I could end up confessing to Michael that I lost our daughter for no reason. I can just picture his smug face.

"So?" Alan asks. "What do you think?"

I close my eyes for a moment. Why did Alice have to run off and make me look like the world's worst mother? I know it's not her fault, though. We should have taken the stairs somehow, like we always do. I'm such an idiot.

"Erika?" he asks again.

I shake the thoughts out of my head and look to Alan. "I'll see you in the lobby," I say, as I start to walk up the stairwell in a hurry. I stop after a few steps up and turn back to Alan.

"What is it?" he asks.

"If you find her, please be extra careful. She's a sensitive little girl."

Alan puts his hands on his hips and stares off into the distance as if I have insulted him. "Erika, I know you don't know me from a bar of soap, but I promise I can help you through this situation."

"I know you will, but it's hard being a mom in this world. You have to understand that she is all I have." We stare at each other for a few seconds before I turn around and start my climb. If Alan finds Alice, I'll do whatever it takes to show him some gratitude. I'll go on the news and tell the world what a hero he is. But right now, I need to focus on locating my daughter.

*

The climb up seems to be taking more out of me than it should. I'm not the fittest person around, but I'm also not this out of shape. The day has already drained me of energy, siphoning the life directly from my soul. Despite feeling like a dead weight on legs, I have to push forward. Alice could be just up the next landing, crying and alone, waiting for me to pick her up and tell her everything will be okay.

If I do find her, I'm ninety-nine percent sure that I'll end up taking her straight home and not carrying on up to retrieve her toy. I'll buy her a new one instead. This day will have taken a lot out of my Bunny. There's no reason she needs to see Michael and me arguing, on top of being lost for longer than I'd ever imagined losing her for.

The floors go by in a blur. Ten, eleven, twelve, thirteen. Finally, I see the top level. Alice's absence is a lump in the back of my skull. How could I have not found her yet?

I open the unlocked door and step out onto the luxurious top floor. The corridor up here is wider and lined with quality materials and surfaces. There are only four massive apartments on this floor. Each has one quarter of the H pattern all to themselves.

I step to the side and lean against the wall for a moment to rest. There's little point knocking on Michael's door without any air in my lungs.

I take thirty seconds to catch my breath and wipe the sweat from my brow. I must look like hell by now—more so than when I first entered Stonework Village. But it doesn't matter how I look. All that concerns me is finding Alice. Michael can help me do that. He lives here, after all, and knows who can be of use. He has to be home. I need him now, more than I have in a long time.

There's no way he'll start fighting with me while Alice is still missing. Instead, he will carefully note down every mistake I have made and use it against me once his daughter has been located. It's just the way he operates these days. We are locked in an endless cold war. I don't care, though. He can make me look like the bad guy all he wants, as long as we find Alice.

I push myself off the wall and make my way over to Michael's apartment: 1402. I'm sure not owning 1401 drives his ego to work more and more hours at the office despite each of the apartments being the same size. I can't even imagine how much this place must cost. I lived in this building for a short while, when we first had Alice. The entire time, I had no idea what the cost of the mortgage might be. Michael insisted upon handling our finances. He managed everything. All I knew was that Michael made more than enough to cover our expenses by charging clients hundreds of dollars per hour for his services.

I find 1402 and stop in front of the door. I close my eyes for a moment and take in a big breath of air before slowly releasing it back out of my mouth. My doctor taught me this trick as a way to reset my emotions and face people with a clean slate. Who knows if it works or not? I never know what people truly think of me.

I knock on the thick timber door three times and stand back a little to straighten myself up and fix my hair as best I can. Part of me still wants to impress Michael. Old habits die hard, I guess. I wait roughly ten seconds and knock three times again, bashing harder. "Come on," I say. "Please be home."

No response.

Maybe Michael really isn't home? I run through it in my head, knowing that he should be here. I made sure we came here on a Sunday morning, after he was due to get back from playing tennis with his busty instructor. He should have been trying to relax for a few hours before another week of soulless bloodsucking began again.

"Michael?" I call out.

"He's not in," says a voice to my side. I turn to see a tall, elegant woman in her late thirties coming down the hall. She must be one of the top-floor dwellers, based on her appearance. She's wearing a white dress with a sleek woolen coat. She moves confidently in six-inch heels, her matching handbag dangling carefree by her side.

"Have you seen a little girl around four years old on this floor?" I ask as I take a desperate step toward her.

"Not today, I'm afraid."

"What about Michael? Do you know where he is?"

"Out. He won't be back for a few hours," she says, coming to a stop in front of me. Her height in heels forces me to look up. I wonder if she has a driver waiting down below to whisk her away to brunch. More importantly, I wonder how she knows so much about Michael's comings and goings.

"How do you know he's out?" I ask. Has Michael been sleeping with this woman? I guess it doesn't matter if he has, but I still hate the thought of it.

She gives me a smirk as she looks me over, silently judging my appearance. She knows I don't belong here, on this level. At best, I could maybe get away with being a resident of one of the lower floors.

"I'm his neighbor, Camille Tessier," she says. I'm unsure how that answers my question. She offers me her hand like I am supposed to know her name. I accept it and give the quickest handshake possible.

"And who might you be?"

"Um, Erika. Michael's ex-wife."

This bit of information raises Camille's perfectly sculpted brows up. "Ex-wife, you say. And you are looking for a little girl?"

I shuffle on the spot, remembering I don't have time for this conversation. "Yes. My daughter's gone missing and I need to see Michael, right away. He might know how to find her. Do you know where he has gone out to? He's not answering his cell. It's important I speak with him."

"Darling, I'm sorry to hear your daughter is missing, but I'm just his neighbor."

I cross my arms. "A neighbor that knows he won't be back for a few hours."

Camille smiles tightly, as if she is actively trying to suppress her emotions to keep her makeup perfect. "It's not like that, unfortunately. Don't think I haven't tried. I know that Michael is out because I saw him leave earlier this morning. We chatted in the hall. He said he had to rush off to an important meeting for a few hours."

"A meeting?"

"You know yourself that he's a lawyer. Surely it's not all that surprising for him to take off on a Sunday for work?"

"No, it's not," I mutter. I don't have time for these games, but my mind throws itself back to the countless Sundays I spent alone with Alice when we should have been out enjoying life as a family of three. Michael would eventually come home, only to spend time with Alice and not me. The divorce came a mere six months into our daughter's existence, but he worked most of that time. We never had the family life I always dreamed of.

"Now, if you don't mind, I must be on my way, dear." Camille turns to leave.

I am left feeling more panicked than when I arrived. "Wait a second," I say to her.

Camille lets out a huff. "What is it? I don't have any more time to waste."

I don't either, I resist saying. "Can I borrow your phone to make a quick call to Alan?"

"Alan? Alan from this building? What possible reason would you have to call that old busybody?"

"He's been helping me search the building."

Camille chuckles. "Darling, please tell me you haven't fallen for that neighborhood-watch line he's always spouting?"

Sweat stings my brow. "What?"

"Oh no, he's gotten to you, hasn't he? Alan's not the head of the neighborhood watch. That's just a lie he tells people. He used to work in the building as the head of maintenance. He got a big payout after they forced him to retire."

Maintenance. Maybe that's where I'd seen him before. Why did he not tell me that to begin with?

"Now he lives here," Camille says. "Pathetic, isn't it?"

I ignore her snobbish statement. "How do you know that?"

Camille's face drops into a scowl. "Because, dear, I know who my neighbors are. Just like the felon who lives on the seventh floor, near Alan. He has been trying to hide his criminal past from the rest of us. I'm pushing for the board to have the man removed as soon as possible. Unfortunately, they have no choice but to keep his identity a secret, but I'll find out soon enough. I mean, how can such a person even afford to live here, anyway?"

The thought of a criminal living on the floor Alice disappeared on sends pins and needles to my fingers. I ask the only question I can as a tremor shudders through my whole body. "Does Alan know about this person?"

"Of course he does. I suspect that he is possibly helping the man to hide his true identity, but I can't prove it."

I shake my head with one hand on my skull. "Why would he do that? Why would he help a criminal?"

Camille lets a sigh flow from her perfect lips. "Alan is nothing but a compulsive liar who is desperate for attention. If he's helping you find your missing girl, I'd just as soon ask someone else to do it instead."

Without another word, Camille walks off toward the elevator, leaving me speechless.

CHAPTER 8

Camille is gone, having dropped the confusing piece of information that Alan is not really the head of the neighborhood watch but is instead a compulsive liar and possibly helping his felon neighbor to hide his past. What have I done? We shouldn't have split up. I shouldn't have trusted that old man so quickly. I always do this. I always believe people. What kind of danger have I put Alice in? And what about this criminal living on the seventh floor?

I need to get to a phone as soon as possible and call the police. I stumble toward the next apartment on the top floor.

I bang on the door of 1403 several times, my fist thumping loudly and rapidly. I realize after a moment that no one would be expecting a knock on their door. They would have someone call them on the intercom first. The only people with this kind of access would be the maintenance team or Henry. Even if anyone is home, they'll look at me through the peephole and decide against opening up to the crazed woman interrupting their Sunday. What was I thinking? I need to keep moving, but I have one other idea left.

Desperate, I call out to whoever might be home. "Hello? I need to use your phone. My daughter has gone missing in your building. She's only four years old. Please help me. I need to call the police."

I keep knocking. No one makes a sound. Are they home? Are they pretending to be out to avoid me? It doesn't matter. I give up and head for the stairwell again.

I need to go back down to the lobby and see if Alan is there with Alice. All I can hope is that Camille was either lying to me or that she has been misinformed. I am so wired up with thoughts of Alan and the criminal he lives next to that the only way I will silence the voice in my head is by rushing back to the lobby. I don't have time to check each floor for Alice. He might have her.

I push through the stairwell door and charge down the first flight of stairs. If Alan isn't the head of the neighborhood watch, then why did he tell me he was? What kind of person lies like that? I feel sure I've led Alice into the hands of a dangerous man, like the gullible idiot that I am.

I stumble down one step, but regain my footing, breaking the thoughts rattling around inside. Alan wouldn't harm Alice, right? He didn't seem the type. Then again, most criminals don't look like criminals, do they?

I catch sight of my face reflected in a big, blurry metal sign that shows the fire exits on each floor's landing. I can still see how much of a disgrace I am, but I keep moving, taking the steps two at a time. The level numbers whiz by in a countdown as I spiral toward the lobby.

I don't know what I will say to Alan. Should I just come out and tell him that I know the truth? That I know about the lies, and the criminal he's helped to hide? Or do I play along and see what he's really up to? But what if that's not the truth? Either way, it doesn't help me to find Alice. She's the only one I truly care about in this mess. If I see her there in the lobby, I'll scoop her up and leave without another word. I don't need to get involved in any drama going on in this building. If she's not there, I'll use Henry's phone at the front desk and call the police. Too much time has been wasted.

A thought grabs me and slows me down: Alan used to be the head of maintenance here. Could he have tampered with the elevator to make it stop on a floor with only a few occupants?

A level he lives on with a criminal? What possible reason would he have to do that?

I shake off my paranoid thinking and reconcile the two facts as coincidental. An old man like that would have no business taking a little girl. I know there are some freaks out there in this dark world of ours, but Alan isn't one of them. I try to convince myself of this. Surely my assessment of him wasn't so far off base that he could be a child abductor? Maybe Camille was messing with me. She did just spew out a lot of gossip to a complete stranger. How often were such dark rumors ever true?

I reach the lobby and throw myself out into it. I stare around the empty floor only to find Henry standing at the reception desk alone. I feel my chest tighten as I rush out into the open space. Where is Alan? He should be here by now. Did I go right by him when he was checking a floor on his way down? Where the hell is Alice?

I rush toward Henry, knowing I need him to call the police. Do I tell him about Alan or keep my fears to myself? Alan was all too keen to get involved in my problem, considering we don't know each other apart from the possibility of passing each other by in the corridors of this building several years ago. The only thing keeping my head on straight is a single question: why? Why would anyone in this place want to take Alice from me?

"Miss Rice? Did you find your daughter?" Henry asks as he sees me. He gives me a professional face full of concern. I rush toward him and plant two hands flat on the counter. I'm out of breath.

"What is it?" he asks me.

CHAPTER 9

I stare Henry in the eyes. "I need you to call the police, right now."

"The police? Are you sure about that?"

"Yes," I blurt out. "Please call them now. I want Alice found."

Henry nods sharply as he lifts the phone to his ear and dials the police. I stand back and feel a wave of heat attach itself to my skull. The reality of Alice being abducted beats me in the face like a crowbar. I've let this happen on my watch. My only child may be in the worst danger of her life and it's all my fault. My lungs begin to suck in air via short, rapid breaths as my chest continues to tighten.

"I'm on hold for the moment. There's some sort of automated message about a delay."

"A delay?"

"I'm not sure what it means, but you should take a second to calm down. You look as white as a ghost. Why don't you splash some water in your face in the restroom while I wait to get through?"

"Okay, fine, I will," I say, "but you need to get through to the police as soon as possible."

Henry nods at me. "I'm connecting now. Yes, I need the police. A child has gone missing at Stonework Village." I listen as Henry continues to describe the situation in full. He relays to me that the police will send a few officers to the scene as soon as they can. He places the phone down and lets out a long breath.

Henry scratches his head for a moment and faces me. "Miss Rice, I seriously think you should go to the restroom and freshen up. You'll feel better for it. Trust me."

"Okay," I say, both hands raised. He won't let up until I do what he wants me to. It's not the worst idea in the world, either, so I turn and walk toward the restroom. I glance back to reception and see that Henry is watching me. He gives me a quick smile for reassurance, which I cannot return.

I pull open the door that leads to the male and female restrooms. No one is around. Inside the female restroom, I find the nearest stall. Once I make it in and take a seat, I close my eyes and remember to breathe. How did this day take such a dive?

The headache I came here with has tripled in size. Everything that has been forced upon me today has only amplified its power. How could I have let any of this happen to Alice? I should have taken the stairs when she asked. I should have been more organized and not worried about some silly doll in the first place. I failed her.

I push up to my feet before fatigue claims me. I don't want to go back out there and face the world when I could stay in here and continue to criticize my actions. But I have to move. I have to keep trying. There will be time to blame myself for everything once Alice is found. For now, though, I have to keep fighting for her. No one else will.

I go to the sink and run the tap, dully staring at my reflection in the mirror. Two flat eyebrows cut across my forehead in straight lines. I look broken. Shattered by the fact that my little girl is out there alone.

I think about the felon on the seventh floor. I should have asked gossiping Camille what crime the man had committed that had landed him behind bars. If he was trying to hide it from the world, how severe a violation was he put away for?

Without knowing what wrong the man had committed, I can only imagine something awful in my head. I try to forget the terrible possibilities and concern myself instead with why Alan would help out an ex-con like that as willingly as he would help a semi-stranger like me to find my missing child. He was the only one to volunteer earlier, while the rest of the people in the lobby preferred to watch the drama unfold.

I leave the restroom and walk back to the door that opens out into the lobby. I open the door slightly to see Henry sitting down and on the phone again. Is he checking in with the police? Had he forgotten to mention something before?

"The situation is under control," he says quietly into the receiver, glancing around the lobby. Henry pauses for a few moments, then nods. "Yes, she's in the restroom now. I'll make sure she doesn't bother anyone."

I don't move a muscle as I listen to Henry's conversation. Who is he talking to? His boss? It must be. I suppose he had to report the police call up the chain to avoid any problems. I don't know if I should feel offended or not that he ushered me off to the restroom so he could complain about me to his superior.

Not wanting to let Henry know that I was eavesdropping, I close the door as quietly as possible and wait a few moments before I loudly open it again. Henry swivels in his chair and stands, placing the phone down a moment later.

"Did that help?" he asks me.

"A little," I say, as I watch him shift uncomfortably. "Do you know how long it will be before the police arrive?"

"Not exactly. I'm sorry. They sounded frantic, but I'm sure someone will be here soon."

He isn't sure? What did he mean by them being frantic? I try to show him I understand as my chest begins to squeeze inward. Air struggles to make its way into my lungs while a tightness grabs hold of my shoulders. Before I know it, I'm stumbling back and tripping over my own feet.

"Are you okay?" Henry asks. The possibility of a lawsuit must be ever present in his mind.

"Alice?" I whisper. "Bunny? Where are you? Come to Mommy." I feel the power drain from my legs as they buckle. Two arms wrap themselves under my armpits and lift me off my feet. I am guided behind the reception desk to a chair on wheels. Henry offers me a drink of water from a bottle that he has tucked behind the counter. I take it with shaky hands and spill some liquid down my throat. What just happened to me?

"Are you okay?" he asks me, over and over. All I can do is stare. I'm beyond useless. Alice would be better off without me.

"Miss Rice? Are you okay? Please, talk to me."

"I'm okay," I mutter. "I'm okay. Just get the police here to find Alice. They have to find her."

Henry nods at me. "Okay. They'll be here soon, I promise you." He would agree to anything at this moment to keep me calm. I can see it in his eyes.

"Thank you," I say. I think about Alan and try not to assume the worst. Maybe he is just taking his time to reach the lobby. Maybe the felon on seven is just a man trying to start over. Perhaps Camille is just a gossip. Alice is simply missing, having gone on an adventure on her own. It wouldn't be the first time she's run off on me. The thought brings me to a state of relative calm after a few moments. It doesn't last.

"Henry?" I ask.

"Yes," he says, his eyes locked on to mine, as if my every word is of the utmost importance.

"What do you know about Alan? And what do you know about the criminal who lives on the seventh floor?"

Henry steps back a pace. "Criminal on the seventh floor? What are you talking about?"

"Never mind," I say, absorbing his reaction. What was I thinking? I came close to accusing a sweet old man of child abduction. I was about to claim that he conspired with some former criminal on the seventh floor to take Alice away from me. How would he have known I was even coming here today with her? No one did.

Henry looks me up and down with a raised brow, cutting through my thoughts. "I figured Alice would have been found by now, but I'm sure she'll turn up soon. Kids have a tendency to run off when they shouldn't, don't they?"

I frown at him. I know he is just trying to reassure me everything is okay, but I don't want to hear it right now. I want to find Alice.

"Miss Rice?" Henry asks.

"Sorry?" I say.

"No, don't worry."

I wave him off and try to regain some strength. I look up and see he has something he wants to ask me. It's itching to come out.

"What is it?"

Henry loses his confidence for a moment as he struggles to speak. "I wanted to talk to you about Alan."

My heart skips a beat. Is there something Henry knows about Alan? "What about him?"

"Well, the thing is, he isn't answering his cell. I was wondering if you knew why. I know he was helping you to search for your daughter. Did he go back to his apartment? I've tried calling him a few times now."

"I don't know what to tell you. He's somewhere up there, looking for Alice." The voice in my head still questions his motivations. Alan's face swirls around in my head. Did Alan know I was coming here? Was his volunteering all part of the act to abduct Alice? He sent me off in the wrong direction, only to disappear. The idea sounds more and more insane every time I think about it. I have to stop thinking this way. The only way to stop my brain from running around in circles is to go back up and find Alice.

"I need to go." I jump to my feet and walk away from Henry to the stairwell, dropping his bottled water in the process.

I decide it's time to search the seventh floor without any outside influence. I'll search the rest once I've made certain Alice isn't up there. She is probably just missing and nothing more. There's no reason that Alan or some criminal would take her.

I try to push the worrisome ideas out of my head. All I can hope is that Alice has ended up in one of the apartments up there and is waiting for her mother to find her and take her away. Otherwise, I'm going to have to come to terms with a suspicion that has been itching in my brain for the past few minutes. I can't bring myself to think it, but it comes out on its own.

What if Alan and this criminal really have taken her?

CHAPTER 10

Then

My pregnancy failed to improve. After the three-month mark, my morning sickness had gotten worse. It should have eased up a little by then. The stress of it was beginning to take its toll on my body.

I was also starting to show, to the point where I could no longer hide the fact if I wanted to. Instead of covering up, I embraced my bump. I was proud of the little bundle of joy that was growing inside me. Proud and scared at the same time. I couldn't wait to meet the tiny person who would, in my mind, look like a perfect balance between Michael and me. But I also stayed awake at night, fearing how I would get through labor when the time came.

We had no idea of the sex then, and had to wait another month to find out. I secretly wished for a girl, while Michael was confident it would be a boy. He spoke about his son all the time, as if there were no possibility the baby would be a girl. Either way, I didn't care. I just wanted a healthy child to hold in my arms and love forever.

I was at home, having quit my job as Michael suggested. I felt uncomfortable doing it, but I guessed he was right. I was taking on a lot of stress without meaning to, which would only serve to harm the baby. I couldn't explain why, but I was constantly on edge about the whole pregnancy. I seemed to be my own worst enemy when it came to being nervous about a situation.

Resting on the two-seater in our old apartment in Brooklyn, I was constantly thinking about the big move we had planned. It was another thing in my life that filled me with dread, and which I couldn't avoid. Our current one-bedroom place suited our former child-free lifestyle, but with the little one on the way, we needed more space to live.

Michael was commuting to his new firm each day for over thirty minutes, while I stayed in the cramped apartment. There wasn't much to do in the small space, so I usually went out whenever I could, despite Michael wanting me to stay home as much as possible and rest. Being stuck in the apartment was its own kind of stress, which could only be fixed by escaping to the world outside.

One day, I was researching nearby schools and daycare options for when we moved to the new place in Brooklyn Heights as we'd discussed. I was also hoping to get back to the workforce when the baby was old enough—not for the money, but to show Michael I could contribute. I couldn't be unemployed like this forever. It wasn't in me to show our child that only Daddy worked while Mommy stayed home.

We'd found several apartments in the area that suited our new budget and lifestyle. I had my eyes set on a few brownstones that were child-friendly while capturing that old-style charm of the city. The neighborhood was the perfect place to raise a family.

Michael had talked about moving to the Upper West Side one day, but I doubted his firm was suddenly going to give him some big promotion after such a short time. I waved off the idea every time it came out of his mouth. Anyway, I didn't want to be part of the wealthy elite, with our own private driver. I just wanted a place that felt like home.

I grew up out in the suburbs of Rhode Island. I would do anything to take our baby to live in that carefree region, but

Michael loved the city too much to move another inch in the wrong direction. I shouldn't have been surprised by his desire to reach the pinnacle of New York living. He'd grown up in the Bronx and only ever imagined himself working his way out of the area and into Manhattan. I tried to tell him he didn't have to work so hard to impress me, but he wouldn't listen. What I really wanted was for him to spend more time at home, with me and the baby.

But Michael was never happy with where he was at the time. He always thought about where he should be and how he could get there. I wasn't sure if it was a byproduct of being a lawyer in a firm filled with ruthless sharks or if he genuinely desired that life for himself and our unborn child. All I could hope for was that when this baby arrived, he would settle down and remember there was more to being a parent than making a lot of money.

I dropped into a daycare center to inspect what the facilities and the staff were like. Michael had told me not to bother looking at any options as we would never need childcare with me at home all the time. While I appreciated the idea of always being there for my child, I also wanted to show our baby that both parents worked hard in and out of the home. It was nice not having to worry about money or commuting each day on the subway, but I also missed the social interaction.

I had worked in a corporate office in Lower Manhattan doing administrative duties. The job itself was boring and repetitive, but I loved the personalities there. They were the main reason I'd stayed as long as I had. When Michael convinced me to leave, I knew it wouldn't take long for me to wish I hadn't agreed to the idea. I missed the job every day, despite not having the anguishes that came along with the territory.

I arrived at the daycare, which was located on the first level of an old church. There wasn't much space in the neighborhood, so daycares were often built wherever they could be. The location didn't concern me. I used to go to church a lot in the past, but had half given up on the idea of religion when I became an adult. The people running the daycare had decorated the rooms in such a way that you had no idea it was ever anything else.

"Hello, Erika," one of the staff members of the facility said, as she met me for a guided tour. We shook hands and walked through the building. I was shown all of the areas the children would be using and fell in love with the place in an instant. Some kids were playing with paints as I went through. I took the opportunity to practice my happy adult voice. It was something I needed to get used to.

"Hello, there. What are you working on?" I asked a little girl with several teeth missing.

"I'm painting my mommy and daddy," she said proudly. I could just make out the blobs of color that represented the nuclear family of two parents and two children.

"That's very pretty," I said as I squatted down.

"Do you have a baby in there?" she asked, before I could call out anything else I liked about her painting. I looked down to see her pointing at my belly. My bump was hardly noticeable. I was impressed she could even see it.

"Why, yes, I do."

"I remember when my mommy had my brother in there. He took a long time to come out."

"Did he now?"

"Uh-huh. And when he did, he had to stay in the hospital for a while to get better."

My mind flicked to the many possibilities of pregnancy and labor. It was terrifying, knowing that anything could go wrong at any time during the entire ordeal. This little girl didn't mean any harm, and I was generally capable of putting such thoughts out of my head until someone mentioned it, but lately, I could only focus on the 'what ifs' that kept me up late at night. I would conjure up the most ridiculous thoughts on what might go wrong during childbirth.

"Did he get better?" I dared to ask, while the staff member stared at me to stop interacting with the little girl like she was poisonous. I shrugged and refocused.

"Oh, yeah, of course. Mommy told me he would. Mommies know best."

"They do, don't they," I replied. What else could I say?

"That's enough, Chantal. Mrs. Walls needs to see the rest of the building."

"No, it's okay. Chantal can tell me all about her mommy if she wants. She sounds like a clever lady."

"She is," Chantal said, in as convincing a voice as a little girl could muster.

I chuckled and gave her a few more minutes to tell me her life story while the daycare worker grew more impatient.

"Well, I'd better be going, but thank you for your time, Chantal. You enjoy your painting, okay?"

"I will. Are you going to stay for story time?"

I glanced at the staff member. "Is that okay? I'd love to see how it all works."

"Sure. Why not?" she said with a shrug. I guessed the typical prospective parent didn't get this involved in the place on a visit.

I sat back as the kids all gathered around in a small circle. There weren't many of them, but I liked the small-group approach. It felt less intense for all involved. It was better than being thrown in with a vast number of children.

The other daycare worker pulled a book from the small library they had on hand. "Today we are going to read an old book called *Alice's Adventures in Wonderland*."

I listened along with the children, smiling as I paid attention to every word and detail. I remembered reading the story as a child and loving it.

Before I left, I put down a non-refundable deposit with a rough timeline for when our child would use the facility. I didn't need to see any other places. My child would go here and grow up in the neighborhood. He or she would come to this building one day and be read that book and make paintings to show off our perfect family.

When I left the building, I was surprised to see Michael hopping out of a cab in front of me. "Honey?" I asked. "What are you doing here?" My heart thudded in my chest.

"I could ask you the same thing. Why are you wasting time looking at this dump?"

I glanced around the street and back to him. "Did you follow me here?"

"No. I saw the appointment written on your calendar this morning. I came here to make sure you didn't put any money down on this place."

"And what if I have?" I asked with crossed arms.

"Then you've wasted a deposit, because there is no chance our kid will ever go here. They won't need daycare." He grabbed me by the elbow and dragged me toward the idling cab. Had he paid the driver to wait? What the hell was I witnessing?

"What are you doing?" I asked.

"Taking you home. You shouldn't be out, getting stressed like this. You should be at home, taking it easy. You need to think of the baby and not just yourself, for a change."

"Are you serious?" I asked. I'd never seen this side to Michael before. The pregnancy and his new job were starting to do strange things to his personality. Did he even see me as anything more than the place where his baby was growing? I didn't like it.

"Stop, Michael. I'm not getting in that cab with you."

He released me the second I told him to. "I'm sorry," he said, stepping back from me. Had he snapped out of some kind of insane trance?

"You should be. I don't appreciate you keeping tabs on me. It's weird. It's not like you to do this."

He shook his head. "I know. I'm just so worried about the baby. And you, of course. And when he or she comes along, I don't want you shoving our child into daycare, just so you can go back to that job of yours. There's no point."

I let out an audible huff. "There is a point, Michael. One you cannot see. I miss working. I don't want to be one of those people who has a baby and gives up on their previous life, okay? You're just going to have to deal with it."

He stared me down in silence and lowered his head. I could see some remorse in his eyes. "I'm heading back to work. Can you please just promise me you'll take it easy for the rest of the day?"

"I'll go home right now if you promise never to pull anything like this again."

His eyes focused on the sidewalk, avoiding me at all costs. "I'm sorry. I don't know what came over me. I'll never do anything like this ever again."

CHAPTER 11

Now

"What are you doing?" Henry asks me as I head to the stairwell entrance.

I shake my head at myself for not realizing he would follow me. I can't tell him about Alan, can I? He doesn't know the situation enough to believe me. At least not until I have some proof.

"I'm going back up there to find her. I can't sit around waiting for the police. She needs me now."

"Are you sure that's a good idea? The police will want to talk to you when they arrive. At least give me your cell number so I can call you."

I stop and turn to him. "I lost my phone up there. You won't be able to reach me."

Henry lets out a huff. "Fine. Take this, if you insist upon going." He pulls an old cell phone out of his pocket. It's not the one that had distracted him so much when I arrived. That must have been his personal cell.

"Thank you," I say, as I take it.

"Please don't lose it. It belongs to the company. The passcode is five four three two. If Alice shows up, I'll let you know, okay?"

"Got it," I reply as I pocket the device. "Is that all?"

Henry huffs at me and shakes his head. "I'll buzz you through the door when you're ready. Please be mindful of the residents with your search. They pay good money for their privacy."

"Fine." I fight the urge to roll my eyes at him. I don't care if I have to annoy every person in the building. I am going to find Alice or someone who knows why she suddenly disappeared, someone like Alan.

*

I open the stairwell door to the seventh floor and see the empty corridor staring back at me. Left or right, the path appears to be the same. Repeating layouts of support columns pressed against the walls and apartment doors line the way, shrinking in size down to the end of the corridor. I don't know which direction to go in, so I start by walking right.

I don't have time to wait for the police to arrive. It will be too late by then, especially if my suspicions of some kind of foul play against my Bunny are correct. The thought stings my eyes and sends a shiver down my spine that I can't shake. I've already lost too much time because of Alan screwing with me. He sent me on a wild goose chase, knowing that I wouldn't get very far. Was that part of the plan? I bet he didn't account for Michael's neighbor being around to spill the beans. What would have happened if I hadn't run into her? Thank God she was there.

I knock on the first door in a hurry, shuffling on the spot as I call out. How many apartments are there on this floor alone? How long would it take me to knock on every door in the building? I don't care. I'll do whatever it takes. I pound the wood again and again, but hear no response. No one shouts out that they are coming. I move on to the next number.

I knock on a few more doors and get no response. Alan must have been telling me the truth about the lack of occupants in this level. I know he lives on this floor, but what I don't understand is why he would be privy to such information. Is he still keeping notes on the building and who lives in each apartment? It seems kind of odd that he would do such a thing.

I keep knocking, calling out and waiting. I get the same silence in return, until I've almost reached the corner and can hear sounds of life inside one of the apartments. I knock on 707 and listen as a person inside responds to my interruption. A man is muttering away to himself like I've spoiled his entire day. Again, I tell myself that people don't knock on apartment doors in a building like this. Even in these lower levels, reception calls or buzzes their intercoms, and I don't fit the profile of someone who has business being halfway up a building crammed full of private residents. I need to keep as calm as possible. Easier said than done.

I see the light blank out on the peephole of the door. I've missed my chance to hide away from whoever is inside the apartment, currently staring at me and sizing me up. The door creaks open a few inches. A bald man lowers his head from up high and levels a single eye out to get a proper look at the person who has disturbed his sanctuary.

"Who the hell are you?" he asks me, his voice muffled slightly by the door.

I stare, like a deer in headlights, my mouth agape. I pray he doesn't yell at me. "I, uh—"

"Out with it. What are you selling? What's this about?"

"Nothing."

"Nothing?" he asks. I can see his thick brow rising with concern.

"No, I mean, I'm not selling anything. I'm—"

"Then what? You're clearly not supposed to be here, so speak your business or leave me alone."

My eyes close as I try to block out his anger. I can feel it spilling out of the apartment, radiating into the corridor. I fight against it despite the dizziness it causes me, not letting this man slow me down.

"I'm sorry to bother you," I say, exhaling. "I'm trying to find my little girl. She went missing on this floor. Have you seen her?"

The man's expression shifts in surprise at the very mention of a little girl. He turns his gaze back to his apartment with a snap, as if someone is in there with him, and then faces me again. "What do you mean, 'missing'?"

I don't want to tell him that I suspect people in the building have kidnapped a little girl. It's too much to put out there without any evidence. My dry mouth falls open as my forehead wrinkles. "Missing. Exactly as it sounds. My daughter ran off on me after the elevator screwed up and half opened to this floor. I can't find her anywhere. I was hoping that you might have seen her come by."

The man says nothing and continues to stare at me. His gaze drops to the floor in thought for a brief second. "Did you call the cops?"

"The man on reception did for me. He said they're on their way, but I don't have time to waste waiting for—"

The door slams hard. Even though it was only open a few inches, I felt the blast of his powerful arm. I knock again, as loudly as I can. All I hear in return is a muted "Go away." I step back and try to work out what this man's problem is. Why did he get all bent out of shape all of a sudden?

My hands fly to my face as the obvious comes to mind. Camille's words rattle around in my head. One of Alan's neighbors on level seven is an ex-con. This has to be him. Why else would he freak out at the mention of the police?

I find myself unsure what to do with my discovery. Could this man have had something to do with Alice's disappearance? I try to contemplate again why Alan would risk his own place in this building just to help such a person rebuild their life. Is he a saint, or is he merely after a criminal connection?

I stumble backward and bump straight into someone. I feel two strong arms wrap around me to stop the two of us from falling over.

"Miss Rice. Are you okay?" Henry asks.

"Uh, yeah, I'm fine, thank you," I say, as I stand up on my own and brush myself off. I see the elevator doors sliding shut. I hadn't noticed it opening. I walk a few paces down the corridor to lead Henry away from apartment 707.

"You haven't been answering my cell," he says as he follows.

I pull out his phone and see it is on silent, with several missed calls. I didn't think to check. "Wait a minute. Why? What's happened?"

"The police called me back."

"They called you back?"

"Yes. A dispatcher informed me that there could be a significant delay before any officers arrive."

I close my eyes for a second, trying to understand. "Are you telling me they aren't coming?"

"Not exactly. They are coming, but they've been held up. Apparently, there has been a major gas leak downtown. As many officers as can be spared have been sent to assist with the emergency."

I stare down at the floor and try to contain what's building inside me. How could this day get any worse?

"I'm sorry, Miss Rice, but there was nothing I could do. Unless this situation is worse than it seems, I'm afraid we will just have to wait for them to arrive."

"It is worse, though," I say. I still don't know if I can tell Henry, or anyone else for that matter, about my strong suspicions regarding Alan, and now Alan's neighbor. I have no way of proving that they had anything to do with Alice disappearing, but something in my gut is screaming at me to take notice.

Henry's mouth hangs open as he tries to think of what to say to me. A fine layer of sweat covers his brow.

"Why don't you come back down to reception with me? I'm sure Alice will turn up before the police arrive. Alan will find her."

I brush past him. "No, I can't. I need to find her myself, before it's too late." I head back down the corridor and past the elevator as Henry follows me.

"What do you mean, 'before it's too late'?"

I ignore the question and begin knocking on another section of doors.

"Miss Rice, I can't have you up here harassing our residents like this."

"Harassing? I'm trying to find my little girl."

"It doesn't matter. I can't have you or anyone else banging on doors. Until the police arrive, I'm going to have to ask you to stay put in reception."

I scowl at Henry. "You're joking, right? Do you honestly expect me to go along with that?"

"Maybe it would be for the best."

"How? How is it for the best? If I'm not out looking for Alice, then no one is."

"Alan is still out there somewhere."

"Alan?" I scoff. "Alan was heading down the stairs from here to supposedly search for Alice. He should have shown up in the lobby ages ago."

"I'm concerned about him as well, Miss—"

"I don't care about Alan," I say, cutting him off. "I just want my daughter found."

Henry reaches out a hand to calm me down. I flinch back. "Please don't touch me, Henry. I swear to God…"

"Okay," he says, backing up a step. "It's all good. I just want you to come with me to the lobby so we can talk about everything."

I shake my head at him. What else can I do? Henry is just trying to keep the peace.

"Right this way," he says. I follow after he takes a few steps, shaking my head.

I glance back to apartment 707 and frown at its door. I'll find out who took my Bunny, whether it was Alan or the man who just slammed the door in my face or someone else altogether. It's only a matter of time. God help whoever gets in my way.

CHAPTER 12

I take a few steps toward the stairwell entrance to leave the seventh floor, only to realize Henry is waiting for me by the elevator. I turn to him with a shake of the head. "I'm not taking that thing. It's the stairs or nothing."

"Are you serious?" he asks.

"Yes. I'm not getting stuck inside that malfunctioning box again while Alice is still unaccounted for."

Henry lowers his head and mutters to himself as he walks toward me. "Fine, we'll take the stairs."

"Good," I say, as I push open the door to the stairwell. I walk through and turn to him as a thought hits my mind. "Who's watching reception?"

"Don't worry. The front door is connected to my smartphone. If someone hits the intercom, I'll get a notification. I can look through the small camera in the intercom and speak to them, tell them to go away, or unlock the door. Pretty cool, huh?"

I don't reply. My main concern is Alan. If he has taken Alice from me, could he have left the building while Henry was up here? I still can't decide if I believe he has abducted my little girl, or if she is simply lost somewhere in the apartment complex.

I make my way down the stairs and pick up the pace, not concerned if Henry is keeping up or not. He's the one making me go back down to the lobby when I should be searching the building for Alice. I know it would be quicker for us to take the elevator, but I can't get stuck inside it again. Not with my luck.

I rush down the steps at a hurried stride that leaves Henry at least a full flight of stairs behind. He can barely keep up with me.

"Come on! Get a move on!" I yell up to him.

Henry yells something inaudible down the stairwell. I shake my head in response. I start to descend even quicker, not wanting to waste time waiting on him. If I'm to wait for the police in the lobby, I should get there as soon as possible, in case they manage to find a spare officer who is not needed to help out with the gas leak Henry told me about downtown.

I keep walking with my eyes glued to the ground. I travel down to the fourth floor on autopilot. Then I spot something, sitting there for all to see, splotched on the wall of the fourth floor's landing at hip height: a small circle of blood. The blood appears to be fresh and is low enough for a four-year-old to have left it there. The world slows around me. Something is horribly wrong.

I drop to my knees, mouth wide open. This can't be real. This has to be a mistake. How can there be blood here? "No, Bunny," I say, my voice barely audible. "Please. Not her."

I crawl over to the splat on the wall and touch the liquid that covers a few inches of the rough surface. I let the red substance coat my fingertips, as if I can analyze my findings like a computer. My hand starts to shake as I study the blood "No, no, no," I mutter, as I try to shake off the warm fluid, scuttling backward until I hit the steps behind me. I spin around and try to escape by crawling back up the stairs.

Henry sees me and stares with his mouth open. "What are you doing?"

My stomach twists itself into knots. I hold up my bloodied right hand, gripping it at the wrist with the clean fingers of my left. Despite the firm grasp I have, my hand still jitters and shakes. What have I found? What does this mean? It can't be from her, can it?

Too many questions cry out for answers as I try to rationalize what I've discovered. Maybe the blood belongs to someone else.

That makes sense. But it's at the perfect height for Alice to have hit her head. I can't ignore that fact. All I want to know is how a four-year-old kid could hurt themselves like this. Memories flash into my mind.

I can't help but remember the time Alice cut her hand at the park. My mind slips back to that moment—to the blood. Alice was excited to go burn off some energy at the park. It was the day after a visit with Michael, so she was feeling quite energized and happy. Whenever she saw her father, she had an extra glow about her that lasted for a few days. It both delighted and angered me. Michael barely spent four hours with her on Sunday at his apartment. That somehow made him a hero in her eyes for the next few days.

Where was my appreciation? Where was my lasting impact? I'd taken care of Alice from the day she was born. Nights spent holding her, feeding her, changing her diapers, absorbing her loud cries, tending to her every need on my own. Michael wasn't there for any of that. Even when we were still together, for that brief six months after Alice's arrival, he would barely lift a finger to help his daughter when he got home from twelve or more hours of being away. Sure, he'd come into our room and spend time with his baby girl, but he didn't take care of her the way I did. Instead, he'd just stare at her in her crib, without saying a word to me.

Even now, after the mess of the divorce, I was like a piece of furniture to Alice. At least, that was the way it felt after she got to visit Michael. Eventually, Alice's glowing admiration of her father would fade into the week and vanish. It wasn't until a day or so before the next visit that she would pipe up again, wanting to see her Daddy. But I would always be there for her, and I would never need any acknowledgment for the effort I put in.

We went to a different park than usual that day, as we had found ourselves in a part of town we hadn't been to before. I had some errands to run and used my phone to source a nearby playground that was on the way home. It wasn't as big or as beautiful as the one we frequented where we lived, but it would do.

I checked the jungle gym over with a sweep of my eyes and realized it was for older children. Alice had already beaten me to the punch, though, and was climbing up the slide before I had a chance to change my mind. She was so cheeky about it, too.

"Hop down, Bunny," I said to her. "Take the stairs like everyone else." There were a handful of other people in this particular park. If we were on our own, I would have let her do what she wanted. I felt it was important for her to experiment and not do everything by the book all the time.

Despite my intervention, I still got the look from one of the other moms. She was there with her partner, watching her two kids go wild and scream their heads off. Apparently, that kind of behavior was acceptable, but not Alice climbing up the slide. I couldn't seem to escape the judgment, wherever I went. It was the burden of being a parent in such sensitive times, I figured. People were always so keen to argue or take offense. Some days it was exhausting.

I sat away from the other parents by the trunk of an old tree. It was the perfect place to set up for Alice's fruit time. She called out to me while she played, making sure I witnessed every little thing she did on the equipment. "Yes, I'm watching," I said for the third time, as I continued to cut an orange into slices for her.

"Ouch," I said, when the tip of the blade accidentally cut my index finger. I dropped the knife as the sting of citrus entered the tiny wound. I sucked the blood and harsh liquid from my finger and fished around in my handbag for a Band-Aid, before remembering that they were located in Alice's backpack. I often took a small first-aid kit along with us in case of emergency. I wasn't exactly dying, but I didn't want Alice to see me bleeding.

My little girl hated the sight of blood. Most children did, but she was particularly frightened by the slightest drop and would often faint when exposed to it. I never understood where her fear came from. I guessed some things couldn't be explained.

"Mommy," she called out to me, as I fumbled with the plastic strips to get the Band-Aid on the right way. I always managed to screw the process up. I would make a terrible nurse.

"Mommy," Alice called again.

"I can see you," I lied. "Very nice." I could hear myself getting frustrated. Some days I just wasn't in the mood to be mommy of the year.

"Damn thing," I said, as I realized I had put the Band-Aid on wrong. I huffed out loud and was fishing around for the next one in the pack when a loud scream broke my concentration.

The high-pitched yell could only have come from Alice. Before I knew it, I was on my feet, searching for my daughter. I rushed over to the jungle gym and found her on the ground next to the metal swing. Another child had hit her with the side of the swing, cutting open her hand. The boy was a few years older than my Bunny and knew better than to swing so wildly when younger children were around. He only stopped swinging when I ducked down to Alice's side and scooped her up. I had no idea who was at fault, but I let the kid have it.

"You need to be more careful. She's just a little girl!"

The boy maintained his distance and silence, showing only a fraction of remorse for getting caught. He ran off before I got another word out, straight to his mother. He pointed toward Alice and me, most likely telling her a bunch of lies. I shrunk away as Alice continued to cry in my arms. I didn't have time to deal with that kid, or his mother, who would no doubt dispute the whole thing with me.

I placed Alice down by the tree and got to work fixing up the cut on her hand. It wasn't nearly as bad as it appeared, but my Bunny thought she was dying when she saw the blood flowing over fingers.

"It's okay, little one. You'll be fine," I said, as I covered the cut with a wad of tissues.

Alice sniveled. "No, I won't, Mommy."

"Yes, you will. Look, it's already starting to stop. Nothing to worry about, Bunny."

She sniffed and stared up into my eyes as her shoulders rose and fell. "Do you promise, Mommy?"

"Cross my heart," I said, as I made an X over my chest with my index finger. She didn't seem to believe me, though, so I pulled her in tight for a cuddle. She cried quietly as I closed my arms around her.

"Everything is going to be okay," I whispered into her ear. "You'll see."

CHAPTER 13

I stare at the blood on the wall in the stairwell. I'm still on the ground, propped against the step behind me. The blood is so fresh that I can smell a metallic odor coming from the stain. I glance down and can sense the same fragrance coming from my blood-covered fingers. Why did I have to touch the wall, like a moth to a glowing light bulb? I try to wipe it off on my sleeve, but the red stain won't budge.

Henry crouches down in front of me to get a closer look. We can both see that Alice will need medical attention as soon as possible—if this is her blood.

I know the police have already been called, but I need to update them on the situation. With shaking hands, I pull out the company cell phone from my pocket and try the passcode Henry told me. I enter it wrong too many times and end up locked out of the phone for a minute.

"Dammit," I yell, grabbing Henry's attention. He turns around and sees what I am trying to do, so he takes the phone from my useless hands and gets it unlocked once the minute passes by.

"You need to call the police again," I say, avoiding eye contact.

He nods at me, already knowing what I was trying to do. "I'll ask them for an ambulance too."

"Thank you," I say, as my gaze falls back to the blood on the wall. How did it get there? What happened here? I need to know the answers to those questions, but I am afraid to discover the truth.

I close my eyes, trying to understand how I found myself in this position. Had Alan been chasing after Alice? Did she trip over and hit her head? Surely I would have seen them on my way up, unless…

My mind thinks up all kinds of desperate scenarios. If Alan took Alice, he must have hidden her somewhere near this floor. When I banged on 707, the criminal may then have warned Alan over the phone that I was sniffing around and had called the police. Did my visit cause a chain reaction that sent Alice running off into the stairwell?

How many people are involved in this? What kind of person would want to take a child from their mother? I can't help but let the murky images into my head.

I notice a few droplets of blood leading to the fourth-floor entrance. I stand on two shaky legs and gaze at the trail. My hand has stopped its shaking for now, with the new distraction. By some miracle, I've managed to avoid a full-blown panic attack.

While Henry requests an ambulance, I take in a deep breath and let the air drain from my body through parted lips. I open my eyes back up and start to follow the blood trail one step at a time.

As cautiously as I can, I open the door. I can only imagine that Alice would have been carried at this point if she had hit her head. I have no way of knowing if that is what happened, but the splatter on the wall is at perfect head height for her. The idea makes me want to vomit. I choke on the image in my brain of my Bunny hurt and lifeless. The lump in my throat is enough to cut off my airways. This can't be happening.

I find more drops on the floor and see that the blood continues along into the corridor. I follow the trail the short distance to the elevator.

"Erika?" Henry calls out to me. "Where are you—?"

The stairwell door closes on him, cutting him off. I don't care what he has to say. I only care about my Bunny. I don't want to stumble across a scene I will never forget, but I have to see where this blood leads.

I walk a few paces and stand in front of the elevator. There's blood on the call button. My legs begin to buckle beneath me as I lose feeling in my feet. I stumble and catch myself on the nearby wall as Henry comes through.

"Erika?"

I don't face him. "Someone hurt her," I whisper.

"What did you say?"

I turn and stare at him. "You heard me. Someone took Alice and hurt her. They chased my Bunny into the stairwell and made her trip into that wall." I can feel the tears forming in my eyes, provoked by a mix of rage and fear.

"How do you know that someone tried to take her? And how do you know that blood came from your little girl? It could be from someone else." His voice doesn't sound convincing in the slightest. I can tell Henry is trying to avoid the worst possible scenario from becoming a reality.

"Someone kidnapped her. And I know that blood belongs to her." I stare at the red on my hand. I can sense Alice in the stain. I know this is from her. It sounds insane, but only a mother could ever tell such a thing.

I face Henry as he stands in silence. I notice he is no longer holding the spare cell in his hands. Clearly, he is not going to give it back to me. "Did you update the police?"

"Uh, yeah."

"And?"

"They'll try to be here sooner than planned," he says. "Why don't you come down to the lobby and sit in the back office with me."

"No. She's still here in this building, bleeding."

"I realize that you—"

"No, you don't understand. Look at the call button on the elevator. It's covered in blood. She must have been running from someone when she tripped into that wall. That person picked her up. I need to track them down before it's too late. Before..." I don't dare finish the thought. My brain can't handle it right now—or ever, for that matter. I stare at the floor and feel the world start to spin.

Henry doesn't say a word, as if he can't understand what I'm saying. Something flashes in his eyes. "Maybe this isn't her blood. Maybe she'll turn up soon."

"It has to be her blood. This wasn't here when I walked up to the seventh floor; not until I spoke to that man in 707."

"What man in 707?"

I flick my neck up. "The ex-con," I say, to gauge his reaction.

"Sorry?" Henry asks.

I study his face, attempting to figure out if he is playing dumb. "You know exactly who I'm talking about. Don't pretend that you don't know about the criminal who lives in apartment 707."

He shakes his head. "I don't know what you're talking about. I've only worked here for a month. Who told you there was a criminal living in 707?"

"No one told me," I lie. "I knocked on his door and saw him."

"And you worked out he was an ex-con?" Henry asks with crossed arms. "How, exactly?"

I don't have time for this. "It doesn't matter. I know he is."

Henry huffs. "Even if that were true, it doesn't mean that he would be behind any of this."

"Do you know his name?" I ask.

"No," Henry says. "And neither should you, so drop it."

I can see he is keeping something about the man to himself. He shuffles on the spot and rubs the back of his neck. I'll get it out of him, one way or another.

"God. I'm going to lose this job if anything else crazy happens today," he says, staring at the wall. "There's no way around it." He continues to babble away, so I drown it out as I think to myself.

I run my hand through my messy hair and scratch at my skull as Henry continues to talk to himself. His words no longer sound real to me as I drift in and out. How can things get any worse?

My eyes fall once more to the blood on the call button. Should I ride the elevator and try to locate the blood? I can't go inside that box again, though. Not after this morning. All I can see is the fear in Alice's eyes any time I'm near the damn thing. Now that image is covered in blood.

I press the call button and jump backward, pressing my body hard against the wall opposite the elevator. I can't stand the sight of the reflective surface of the doors, but I need to see inside it. After a short delay, the elevator arrives and opens. It's completely empty, with no traces of blood.

"Come on," Henry says, having pulled himself together. "We need to go back to the lobby."

He grabs me by the elbow and directs me to the stairwell entry. He pushes the door open.

I see the bloodstain on the wall again. "Wait," I say. "We can't just leave the blood like that. It could get contaminated before the police arrive."

"Right," Henry says, lightly slapping his head. "I'll call our maintenance supervisor to put up signs."

I take one last look at the blood as Henry guides me down the stairs. Only one thought clouds my brain: Where are you, Bunny?

CHAPTER 14

Then

It had been a day and a half since I'd last felt the baby kick. I'd been monitoring and counting her movements ever since I reached twenty weeks. She usually kicked a lot throughout the afternoon and into the early evening. She seemed to be most active when I was trying to go to bed on time.

We'd found out the sex of the baby about a month previously. Not wanting a surprise when the time came for our little bundle of joy to arrive in the world, we asked our doctor what we were having. I was over the moon to learn we'd be the proud parents of a little girl in roughly four months' time.

Panic began to set in when I hadn't felt a single kick in a few hours. By the end of twenty-four hours, I was really starting to freak out. On an average day, I could count several hundred kicks or movements. There would be times when she was less active, but this was beyond concerning. It was like she had disappeared. My mind dreamed up all kinds of reasons why she wasn't moving and kicking, and they all centered around me. I must have been stressing out too much, or I'd eaten the wrong thing. My husband would be furious with me.

Michael left work early to take me to the doctors. He seemed even more worried about our little one than I was. In general, he made sure I did everything in my power to stay healthy and stress-free. He'd monitor my diet and exercise like a hawk, bugging me throughout the day with what he thought were helpful text messages. I had to remind him on more than one occasion that I was the one having the baby and not him. He thought he knew best, but Michael wasn't the one who would have to push our daughter out when the time came.

I sat in a small waiting room, anxious to see our doctor. The clinic was a private practice in Manhattan that Michael insisted we use. The specialist we'd come to see was highly regarded and had been present at every checkup since day one. Michael paid through the nose for the service, even with his insurance. It was fortunate he had gotten his new job, which allowed him to cover the ongoing cost of these appointments. I couldn't even imagine what the hospital bill would be like after our baby was delivered.

I held my belly with both hands, desperate to feel a kick or a movement. She had to do something soon. It had been so long since I'd felt her tiny yet powerful legs. I kept moving my hands around to different places, wondering if I had lost the ability to sense her presence. Was that even possible? Since I'd first felt her move, she'd been busy every day, jumping around and kicking me to let me know she was doing well.

"Anything?" Michael asked from the seat next to me. He had a magazine rolled up in his hand. I don't think he'd read a single page, instead flicking through it to try and distract himself.

"No, sorry. I just wish she would do something. I can't take another minute of this."

Michael shook his head. He held out his hand and placed it on my belly. The baby didn't respond. We thought we had special powers as her parents, but nothing we did was making a difference.

"Why won't she kick?" I asked him, as if he were the doctor.

He shrugged and placed the magazine back down on the pile. "I wish I could tell you. I really do." He released a heavy breath and pinched the bridge of his nose with his index finger and thumb. "Maybe she's just feeling a bit lethargic at the moment."

"For this long, though?"

"It happens."

"I know," I said. I'd spent most of the day on the web, looking at forums and articles on fetal movement. I couldn't help myself. It both helped and made things worse. The polar opposite opinions online were enough to drive a person stupid.

I stared at Michael, as his gaze wandered around the empty room. He was deep in thought about something, his eyebrows raised and then crunched down. What was happening inside that head of his?

"How did your boss take it?"

Michael turned to me with furrowed brows. "Sorry?"

"For leaving early today. How did your boss take it?"

"Oh, yeah. Fine. She understands what it's like. She's got three kids of her own. All grown up now."

"Really?"

"Yeah. Crazy, right? Beats me how you raise three kids while building a solid career in law. I guess she's just a natural at it."

I wasn't sure if he meant motherhood or being a lawyer. I didn't want to push for clarification and spoil our conversation. We'd argued time and time again about me quitting my job for the baby. The further along I got in the pregnancy, the worse I felt about the decision. Now, he was telling me his high-achieving boss had managed to have three kids and a successful career without causing her children harm, while I could barely keep out of danger while sitting at home on my butt.

Michael loved to run my life while he worked long hours at the firm. At the moment, he was working anywhere from seventy to eighty hours per week. Sometimes more. He claimed he wouldn't work this much if he had a choice. I didn't believe him, though.

He didn't have to be a top-notch lawyer. It wasn't sustainable, especially once the little one arrived.

I knew that he'd worked hard to get to where he was today, but something had to give if he wanted to be part of a proper family and not just a father who was there for the fun times only. I didn't want to end up raising this child on my own. It was an argument I knew was coming, but which would have to wait for another day. Right now, our baby needed her parents.

Our doctor called us into her office a few minutes later. She was a middle-aged Indian woman with black hair, wearing thick-rimmed glasses that you would find on a woman half her age. She sat me down on a special chair that she could control at the click of a button. Michael sat back in a regular seat, watching the examination unfold.

"How are you feeling?" Doctor Gilliam asked.

"I'm fine," I replied. I was anything but fine, though. My back was killing me, my feet hurt, and I couldn't sleep at night. Michael knew this too, but he didn't say anything.

"It's the baby who's got me worried," I said. "She hasn't moved or kicked in over thirty-six hours."

The doctor gave me one of those looks that filled my body with a gripping fear. I tried to read into what her eyes were trying to hide, but she moved away from me in a hurry.

"Let's take a look and see what's going on."

Within a few minutes, I was lying back for an unscheduled ultrasound. The gel felt cold on my stomach as Doctor Gilliam rubbed the substance over me. I stared up at the cloned monitor above and saw the baby come into view from multiple angles. Something seemed different about her position from the last time we did this.

"I see what's happened. She's moved away from her last position, toward your spine. That makes it hard for you to feel her movements. They do that sometimes."

I leaned up to the monitor. "But she's okay, right?" I asked, sounding desperate.

"Perfectly fine. Here. Listen." Doctor Gilliam flicked a button on her station and turned a dial. A throbbing heartbeat filled the room, thumping away with perfect rhythm. It was like music to my ears. I slid back down and breathed a sigh of relief as a smile etched its way across my lips.

"Thank you, Doctor," I said.

"Don't mention it. Now, I can assure you everything is fine. Your baby will move forward again soon enough. She is going to do a lot of growing over the next few months. You'll feel her presence a lot more as time goes on."

"That's great to hear, Doctor," Michael said as he stood. "Thank God she's okay." He started walking toward the door.

The doctor ignored his eagerness to leave and refocused on me. "Seeing as you are here, is there anything you are having trouble with? There are a lot of symptoms around this time that can be quite frustrating to deal with."

I wanted to tell the doctor about the various problems that were giving me grief on a daily basis. I glanced over to Michael and saw how desperate he was to leave. He knew I'd been struggling a bit lately, but he didn't seem to want to bring it up now that we had learned that our daughter was okay. As long as the baby was doing well, nothing else mattered.

"Why don't you head back to work," I said to him. "I'll take a cab home after we're done here."

"That would be amazing," Michael said. "I've still got a huge pile of paperwork to get through."

I gave him a feeble smile and said, "I'll see you at home," knowing full well that he wouldn't get in until some late hour and would want nothing to do with me.

Michael didn't need further prompting. He stepped over to me and rubbed my belly. "You scared us, little one. Don't do that again." He thanked the doctor and opened the door. He closed it without looking back as my fake smile faded.

I couldn't believe it, but he left me on my own so that he could go back to work. Would he ever care about me again?

CHAPTER 15

Now

Henry accompanies me down the stairs to the lobby, letting me go first. The stairwell is too narrow to walk side by side, forcing me to be alone with my thoughts.

The blood we found can only mean bad things have happened in this building today. I try not to think about how close I was to possibly running into Alice in the stairwell. If I had come up only a short time later, would I have spotted her trying to escape from her kidnappers?

I know there is more than one person involved in her disappearance. I'm still trying to come to terms with my suspicions about Alan and the man in 707. If anyone has arranged Alice's abduction, it has to be them, right? But why?

I try to push down the possibilities rattling around in my head and hope instead that Alice is simply lost somewhere on a floor I haven't been to, trying in vain to find her father.

Michael flashes into my mind in a way he hasn't this entire time. Several thoughts hit me at once, as I think back to only a few weeks ago, when I sent him a text saying that he needed to do more to support Alice and me. Lately, Michael had been late to pick up Alice. As much as I didn't want him spending time with her, it frustrated me to see her disappointed face whenever he showed up an hour later than scheduled.

It wasn't his punctuality that had me concerned, but his reply: "It's all going to be fine soon. You won't have to worry anymore."

"Oh God," I say, as my legs buckle beneath me. The revelation cripples my body into submission, and I drop to the concrete floor of the final landing before we reach the lobby.

"Miss Rice?" Henry asks. "Are you okay?"

I don't respond. The collar of my top feels tighter than it should around my neck. I tug at it, feeling that I won't be able to breathe unless I get a few fingers into the gap. Painful thoughts fill my brain with doubt. Has Michael arranged for Alice to be kidnapped? Am I really thinking about this possibility? The scenario plays out in my head.

Alan was in the lobby when the elevator screwed up and stopped at seven. The criminal was on the seventh floor where the elevator stopped. They couldn't have been where they were by chance.

Michael had to have been in charge of this whole operation. He must have known I was coming. He just had to orchestrate the right scenario to take his daughter back from me.

He paid the former maintenance man of the building to rig the elevator to stop at a floor where his secretive criminal friend lived. Michael knows how terrified Alice is of elevators, and allowing the doors to open part of the way guaranteed that she would run away from me—right into the hands of a man Michael had paid to abduct her. It had all gone according to plan, except for when they decided to move her around.

"Are you okay?" Henry asks again. "Miss Rice? Please. I need you to get up."

"Okay," I say. "I'm sorry." I glance up to Henry. His eyes are stuck wide open. I bet he never expected any of this to happen when he woke up this morning. Neither did I. How could I have expected any of this? There were signs Michael was up to something, but I never imagined this was what he had in mind.

Henry pulls me to my feet and makes sure I can walk on my own. I shrug him off and continue down the next flight of stairs.

We reach the bottom of the stairwell, and Henry moves ahead of me to open the door to the lobby. The area is empty. No residents are walking around, no police officers are charging in, and there are no paramedics to speak of.

"Follow me," Henry says. "I'll take you to the back office so you can rest up until Alice is found."

"No, I can't. What if she escapes the building?"

"She won't. The front door is locked and can only be opened by a button she wouldn't be able to reach."

"What about the fire exits? She could have gone through one of them."

"No alarms have gone off. I would receive an alert on my cell the second one of them did."

Henry has thought of everything and seems confident that Alice is still somewhere in the building. I hope he's right. She has to be here. I gaze around the lobby and see a few security cameras fixed to the corners. "Do you have access to those cameras? Maybe we could find her on one of them?"

He shakes his head. "The system has been down for a few days. We're still waiting on a technician to come and fix them. I'm sorry."

"It's fine," I say as my shoulders slump. "The police won't be long, though, will they?"

"The gas leak could still be causing some delays. Hopefully, our update to them will get things moving."

I shake my head and silently curse to myself. I know Henry didn't mean anything by the "update" remark, but it's hard not to take offense. My little girl is somewhere in this building, kidnapped and bleeding from a wound that I should be attending to. Instead of helping her, I'm down in the lobby, waiting for the police to arrive.

Henry takes me through a locked door, only accessible via a key card he has tucked away on his lanyard. We walk down a damp corridor and arrive at a small back room which has a kitchenette attached to it. He points out the sink, where I can wash the blood off my hands, and then a hot-water boiler. The unit is connected to the wall above and is bordered by some cheap facilities that the building provides him.

"Help yourself to a coffee. It's just instant, I'm afraid."

"That's fine," I say, as I think about the number of times Michael has sent coffee back at cafés for not being perfect. Did he drink a cup of coffee when he planned on kidnapping our daughter?

"You can relax on this chair here while I hold down the fort. I'll come collect you the second Alice is found. If you need to come back out to the lobby, the door unlocks by itself from this side. There's also a phone in the corner there. Just hit the button labeled 'Lobby' if you want me for any reason."

I drop into the chair and don't respond. My words seem pointless right about now. Alice is still missing, and I'm sitting on my ass about to drink coffee. My Bunny is probably staring at her kidnappers right now, afraid for her life, and I'm deciding how many sugars I should have.

Henry slinks back to the lobby. He simply carries on, business as usual, as do the residents in the building. The whole world goes about its day while Alice slowly suffers.

I pull out a Styrofoam cup from a packet and toss in three teaspoons of the foul-smelling instant granules Henry directed me to. I put in just as many sugars, deciding I need all the extra energy I can get. The hot water splashes over the cup and burns my hand. I don't even feel it. I'm numb to pain. Nothing could hurt me worse than knowing what I know about this day.

I drink the coffee, slurping it down. It scalds my lips and throat with every last drop. I make another one and repeat the process. After the second cup, I can feel my eyes popping with the caffeine hit I've been craving for hours. I silently pray it will do the trick and help me to stay focused. I need to be ready to go the second the police arrive.

The liquid hits my stomach and reminds my body that I need to pee. I've been so focused on finding my Bunny, I'd forgotten to use the bathroom. I wonder, if I had just taken Alice to pee to begin with, would this day have turned out the same? Would Michael still have gone through with what I suspect of him?

I duck out of the room, desperate to empty my bladder. I think about heading to the restroom just off the lobby, but I stop when I see a small toilet sign in the opposite direction. Deciding not to interrupt Henry, I use the staff toilet.

I feel slightly less anxious after using the tiny restroom. I wash my hands and see my reflection in a mirror, which looks like it hasn't been cleaned in years. I swear my appearance has gotten worse since I last looked. I feel like I've aged one year for every minute Alice has been missing.

On my way out, I notice another small room tucked away to the left at the end of the corridor. I'm not sure why, but I travel further into the belly of the building, only to find an office with a light on. There's no one inside, so I venture in—looking for something to keep my mind distracted from the waiting. Every second I have to myself is filled with guilt and worry. I hate this feeling of uselessness that is hovering over me at all times. I despise myself more and more with every second that goes by. Only finding Alice safe and sound will begin to remove this feeling.

I walk into the small room. All I find is an old desk covered in a mess of papers, and a few filing cabinets shoved against a wall. I realize I'm in the office of the maintenance supervisor. I instantly think of Alan and feel a stab of pain hit me in my chest.

"Where are you, Alan?" I ask out loud. I imagine him sitting at this desk, going about his day. Camille said he had been forced to retire from his job. Why? And what would make him want to help Michael commit such a vile crime? What made him team up with an ex-con, of all people? It makes no sense that a man would suddenly take such dangerous risks during retirement. Did he have money troubles? Did Michael promise him the world in return for his part in all of this?

I try to drive the thoughts out of my head, but they don't want to budge. I still have no proof my suspicions are entirely correct, and I can't afford to go off the deep end. But I swear I might if this day gets any worse, and I know that it could.

I rifle through the paperwork on the desk, pushing it aside, unsure what I'm looking at. Why am I even in here? I never imagined when I woke up this morning that I would be attempting to distract myself from such a screwed-up situation by going through boring paperwork. I guess it reminds me of my admin job and gives me some level of comfort.

None of the pile seems all that important. Work orders, supply lists, ongoing issues, budget problems. Boilerplate documents that would put anyone else to sleep within a few minutes.

I'm getting up to leave when I see a face pop out at me from the mess. "What?" I say out loud. It's a photo of the man from 707. The same scowl I saw earlier today stares up from the chaos of paperwork. His picture is attached to some documentation with the name Stonework Village written all over it. I pull the page from the pile and run my eyes over the information. I almost drop the paper when I see the man is an employee of the apartment complex. Not only does he live in the building, he is actually one of the maintenance people who service Stonework Village. How did an ex-con manage that? I thought it was near impossible to get solid work after doing time.

I scan over the paper, desperate to find out who this man is. I can tell the police all about him when they get here. I already know he has a record. My eyes finally land on his name: Desmond Bracero.

"Bracero?" I say out loud. Where have I heard that name before? I try to recall the surname, wondering why it's so familiar.

It sits on the end of my tongue, ready to pop out. Just as I am about to rule it out as an odd bit of information stuck in the back of my brain, it hits me.

"Alan!"

I step back in a rush until I slam into a filing cabinet. "What the hell?" I say out loud. My mind runs wild as I try to make sense of what I have discovered. "Desmond Bracero," I say out loud. "Alan Bracero."

I close my eyes as my world begins to swirl. This explains why Alan would go out of his way to help an ex-con move into the same building as him, and why he would line the man up with a secure job in maintenance.

Alan is Desmond's father.

CHAPTER 16

I escape the maintenance office and rush back to the kitchenette, bumping into walls and doorframes in the process. I need a moment to think straight, to try and absorb the information that Alan is the father of the ex-con in apartment 707. The name Desmond stains my mind as I see a flash of his face through the gap in the door again.

"Shit," I say out loud. My discovery changes everything. It makes me absolutely confident that Alan had something to do with Alice's disappearance. Any doubt has vanished along with his kind old man act. Why Alan seemed all too kind and eager to help makes perfect sense now.

I sit down on a chair in the kitchenette, unsure what to do with my discovery. Alan and Desmond have to be working for Michael. He has paid them to take her from under my nose and make me look like an incompetent mother who loses her daughter. It's the only argument that makes sense.

Otherwise, they have taken Alice for their own reasons. I shake my head as the ramifications of that likelihood set in while my breathing speeds up. If Alan and his son aren't working for Michael, why have they kidnapped an innocent little girl?

The phone in the corner blares out loud, sending my already high heart rate through the roof. I attempt to pick up the receiver, but my hand starts to shake uncontrollably. I grip my wrist with my other hand, determined to answer the call. I know it's Henry, but I don't know what I'm going to tell him. Should I share what I know about Desmond?

I grip the phone and lift it up to my ear. The cheap plastic feels heavier than it should, as a weakness cripples me to my core. I take a breath in and try to center myself to regain a semblance of control. It doesn't work, but I force myself to speak. "Hello?"

"Erika, it's Henry. Is everything alright? You took a while to answer."

"Ah, yes," I say in a panic. I close my eyes as I try to fit my thoughts together in my head.

"Good. I just wanted to let you know that I've had another update from the police."

"Really?" I ask, my voice picking up with hope.

"There's been another delay, I'm sorry. The gas leak has gotten worse and has cut off several streets downtown. They've had no choice but to pull in even more police officers to keep the public back to a safe distance."

I shake my head at my terrible luck. "Okay," I say, defeat crushing my voice.

"I'm sorry about this."

"Not your fault," I say, as my grip on the phone begins to fade.

"They said they'd call as soon as they had something positive to tell me."

"Okay then." I can barely muster up the words to answer him.

"Take it easy, Erika. The police will be here as soon as they—"

"No, wait. If the police aren't coming, someone needs to be looking for Alice."

"I already thought of that. Seeing as Alan is still not answering, I've got someone from maintenance going floor to floor as we speak. They'll find her soon enough."

Maintenance? My heart skips a beat. "Who?" I ask, praying this someone isn't Desmond. He didn't seem to be dressed for work when I saw him.

"His name's Gus. He's the maintenance supervisor. Look, Erika, I gotta go. There's people at the front door begging for me to let them in. Just try and relax. Alice will turn up soon. I promise."

The line goes dead. My mouth hangs open. I drop the receiver back into its home. I feel tears welling up in my eyes. Another delay from the police takes us a step closer to sealing Alice's fate. How can the authorities be taking this situation so lightly? She's four years old, missing, and hurt. The police should be here, gas leak or not. A single maintenance worker isn't the response team I need.

I shake my head again and decide that Henry needs to get someone higher up from the police department on the phone, to make our emergency call stick out among the other mounting problems the city will be facing today. Maybe if he tells them about Desmond, it will move things along.

I head for the exit to the lobby and stop halfway there when something hits me like a smack on the back of my head. Henry is the only one to have spoken with the police. He is the only one receiving updates. I start to wonder a few sickening thoughts that I hope are just stress-related nonsense.

Did Henry pretend to call the police? Did he just call Michael each time to fake the whole thing? Maybe that wasn't his boss on the line earlier.

Then a second thought hits me hard, shoving me against the wall: is there really a gas leak downtown? I have no smartphone on me to find out online. Now I'm being kept out of the way in some dingy back room, cut off from the world.

"No," I whisper. It can't be true. I don't want it to be. I can't bear the thought of another person working with Michael to take my Bunny away from me. She doesn't deserve this. If anything, Michael should be punishing me and leaving her out of our differences. She's the only innocent one in our family.

Just as I am about to lose my mind and run out into the lobby, I hear a faint siren in the distance. At first, I swear it's all in my head. Or it could be the building moaning and groaning as it continues to serve its occupants.

The noise grows louder with every passing second, as if an emergency vehicle is heading for the building. Could it be a police officer?

I move closer to the lobby door and press my ear up to the cold surface to listen. The siren is getting louder and louder. It's coming to Stonework Village. I know it.

I take a breath and shake out my wrists. If that is the police out there, about to come inside, I need to put my game face on. I'll need to move fast and help in whatever way I can.

I turn the handle to the lobby door, but it doesn't budge. The door rattles slightly in response to my jiggling. I try it again, pressing harder. Nothing. This can't be right, I think, as I take a step back. Surely Henry wouldn't lock me in the back room like this? He left me with a working telephone. All I need to do is call the cops.

The thought seems like a good one. I rush back to the kitchenette and grab the phone. I dial 911 and wait for a connection. I hear nothing to indicate the phone can call out. I hang up and try again. Dead air is all I get. Either there is a special button I have to press to dial out, or this phone is only for internal purposes.

I feel a wave of panic envelop me as the siren reaches its pinnacle. It has to be coming for me, coming for Alice. I let the phone hang by my side for a moment as I force myself to think.

"Come on," I say, as I tap the receiver against my head. "Think, dammit." I stare down at the phone and start to try different combinations to dial out.

I try 0. Nothing.

I try 9. Nothing.

I try every other number and button on the damn thing until I hit "Lobby." The phone rings out to Henry. What the hell am I going to say?

"Yes, Erika?"

"What the hell?"

"I suppose you want to know what's going on. Look, I think it's best if you just stay put for now and—"

"Are you kidding me? I can hear the siren. It's coming here, isn't it?"

"Yes, but—"

"But nothing. You've locked me in the back room and won't let me out when the authorities finally show up."

"Sorry?"

"You heard me. The door won't open. You told me it unlocks from this side. It won't open."

"Damn thing must be stuck again. Give me a minute and I'll open it for you." He hangs up the phone. Is this another tactic to give me hope? I honestly don't know who I can trust anymore. I leave the phone on the table and head for the exit to the lobby, hopeful Henry is telling the truth.

The door swings open to reveal Henry staring at me from the lobby. He runs his gaze over me with a furrowed brow.

I try to gauge his body language.

"Erika?"

"No. I have to tell you something."

"Okay," he says, as he ushers me out with one open arm. "Can it wait, though? I'm going to need to talk to these people."

I walk out and see an ambulance parked on the sidewalk in front of the building. My brow tightens at the sight. I was expecting to see a police cruiser instead. I figure the ambulance Henry requested has arrived first. Henry guides me to his chair at reception and tells me to sit for a moment before he unlocks the front door to the lobby. I obey like a dog, while my eyes stay glued to the paramedics as they rush inside. Henry greets the man and woman head-on. I study his face, wondering why he looks so confused to see the EMTs coming into the building. He called them here.

I stand and push the chair back. I'm not going to sit around and wait while the paramedics get the slow version of the day's happenings. I move with purpose toward the three. I have to take action for Alice. She needs to be found, right now, so these people can give her the aid she needs.

The flashing lights of the ambulance slow me down as I reach the group. The swirling beacons send a stab of pain to my core as a memory tries to surface. I shake it off and continue toward the group. I can't let anything stop me now. I will find Alice and get her the help she needs.

CHAPTER 17

The paramedics brush past me in the lobby before I have the chance to say a single word to either of them. Henry tags along by their side. He turns to me. "Stay here."

I come to a stop at his order but then realize I have to keep moving. "No way," I mutter, as the two trained professionals rush for the elevator—as if they know where Alice is. Are they planning on searching the building until they find her? I give chase, determined not to let them out of my sight. I need to be there when they locate my Bunny.

Henry and the two paramedics huddle around the elevator, waiting for it to become functional again. I realize in a flash that the three of them are about to use the faulty elevator. If it fails again, they will get stuck and not be able to help Alice.

Before I can warn them, I see the three cram into the elevator. The doors start to shut straight away as Henry slaps the close button over and over.

"Don't take the elevator," I yell.

Henry tries to wave me back. "Stay there, Erika."

"No, it's not safe. You might get stuck."

"You don't understand. We're going to the seventh floor to—"

The doors seal shut.

"The seventh floor to what?" I yell. I run to the stairwell entry but remember it's locked. I rush back to reception and find the hidden button Henry used to buzz me through. I find a large button and slap it hard. I run back to the stairwell door and slam through without any concern as to who might be on the other side. If I knock some resident over, they'll soon recover. Alice, on the other hand, could have been injured for far too long without receiving any medical attention. Her safety holds more importance than anyone else's in the building right now.

I pull myself up the steps two at a time, yanking hard on the railing. With every corner I round, I can feel the strain being placed on the aging structure. Some rails wobble more than others, their bolts having loosened over time with oily hands and heavy weights.

The floor numbers pass by and my legs ache from the effort I've put them through today. On a busy day, I'd be lucky if I moved around half this much on flat ground, let alone bounding up and down flights of stairs.

Adrenaline spurs me on, blocking the pain my ankles are taking from climbing the stairs in ballet flats. I'd almost be better off doing this climb in my bare feet, but I don't have time to stop and take my shoes off.

What will I say to Alice? Will I be upset with her? Not a chance. Seeing her safe and sound will be all there is to care about. I'll pick her up from the ground and hold on tight. I may never let go of her after today. How can I?

I'm almost halfway there and can feel the drain of the last hour or so pulling me down. The stairwell feels like a giant bathtub full of water that has had its plug suddenly pulled out. I'm being sucked down by gravity's unbiased power, taking me along for the ride. I'm fighting against the current, and I know it.

I reach level four and see the blood drying on the wall. Henry's maintenance man has put up signs to keep people away from it. The sight sends a stab into my chest that radiates down to my core. I almost come to a stop, drawn in by the morbid scene. That blood isn't where it should be. It needs to be back in my Bunny, keeping her heart beating strong.

I force my brain to stay focused on the simple job at hand. I pick up the pace as I reach out for the next railing to propel myself up the steps. I'm so close to level seven I can smell its carpeting. I can hear the hum of the lights. I can picture Alice running down the corridor, fleeing from the paramedics.

"Come on!" I say out loud. I have to be there when they reach her, wherever that is. She'll be too scared to speak. Do they know she goes by the name Bunny? Has Henry told them? Why have I been left out of this? A mother should be the first person to be consulted on any matter concerning a child. No one else knows better.

She grew inside my body. Her tiny hands and feet formed, her heart pumped for the first time, her eyes came to be inside me. No one else knows Alice like I do—especially not her father. He thinks he can just take her from me. But you can't replace a mother's love.

Level seven finally arrives and I open the door with sweaty hands. I struggle to breathe and make myself take a few seconds to collect my thoughts while my lungs play catch-up. I won't be able to help the paramedics with Alice if I'm short of breath and can't speak.

I glance down the corridor and see Henry and the two medical staff enter an apartment I'd knocked on earlier. It's close to the stairwell, but I need the support of the walls to move my legs along to reach it.

I see past the elevator as its doors close. I'm not far behind them, and I wonder if the group had similar problems to Alice and me. I don't see any evidence to suggest their ride was anything other than smooth. It only adds to my theory that someone tampered with the damn thing.

I shake off the past as much as I can and stumble forward. The door to the apartment they all went into is still open. I won't let them shut me out. Not this time. I'm not going to be stuffed into some back room while my daughter suffers. This search for her has taken far too long. How could I let her stay missing like this?

As I reach the door to apartment 702, I wonder why she is in someone else's apartment.

Hopefully, a good Samaritan found her and couldn't stand to see a hurt child wandering around the floor by herself. I picture some dear old lady, whose selfless concern may have saved my Bunny's life. Did this old lady call for an ambulance?

I reach the apartment and clutch at the doorframe as I wheeze for air. I need to fight through the pain in my chest and move inside. I want Alice to see a stable mother who isn't a complete mess when I enter the room and find her there.

I stumble inside and see Henry at the rear of the two paramedics. They are huddled around someone on the floor I can't see, but she's here; I know it.

I take in a deep breath. They've found her. It's finally over.

Henry hears me coming and turns around. "Erika. No, you shouldn't be here." He rushes toward me and stops my approach.

"Let me go," I yell. "She needs me." I try to fight him off, resisting his attempt to keep me from my daughter.

Why is he doing this?

Why doesn't he want me to see her?

My thoughts take a dark turn as the worst thing a mother can fathom enters my brain. "Is she…?" I can't even bring myself to utter the words. She can't be. Not after everything. Not now.

I feel my legs buckle and I begin to fall to the ground. Henry guides me down to the floor, saying words I can't process. Time slows down as I see the paramedics hunched over a body, blood on gauze. They ignore my cries.

"Erika!" Henry shouts through the haze.

My eyes snap up to his.

"You don't understand," he says.

"I do. She's dead."

His gaze hones in tight. "No. This isn't Alice. It's Alan."

CHAPTER 18

Then

"Close your eyes," Michael said to me as we walked along the sidewalk. We had taken a cab all the way to Central Park from Brooklyn and had spent a few hours there relaxing on a Sunday afternoon. I almost had to pinch myself when Michael made the suggestion. We hadn't done anything so exciting on the weekend in months. My husband was always working—at the office or at home. He barely ever had any time for me. He only cared about whether I was eating healthily enough for the baby, and how she was growing.

"Are your eyes closed?" he asked.

"Yes, I promise," I said with a chuckle. We'd taken a quick stroll from the park to get some food at one of the cafés a few blocks away. Michael wanted to take me to a particular place he had told me he'd met a few clients at. Apparently, the food was the best he'd ever eaten, and the coffees were always perfect.

I struggled to see how it could be better than some of the cafés we had around Brooklyn. Just because they weren't in Manhattan didn't mean the staff didn't put as much effort into their food and drinks.

"This had better be good," I said. "It's not fun being seven months pregnant in these shoes, I can tell you."

"Trust me, this will be worth the trip, so keep your eyes closed."

Michael guided me along by the elbow, helping me to avoid tripping over anything dangerous in the busy Manhattan streets. Though my eyes were still tightly closed, I could feel the people around me getting annoyed at Michael's playful idea. I hoped the café wasn't much further. As fun and rare as it was to goof around with him, I was feeling drained of energy, as usual.

"Are we close?" I asked.

"Almost there."

"This is crazy," I said. "People must think we're insane."

"Who cares? Let 'em stare."

"I knew they were all gawking at us."

Michael snorted. "They wouldn't be staring if they had any idea what I'm about to show you and our baby girl."

As if on cue, our daughter kicked as hard as she could. I didn't know what to make of Michael's comment. It seemed an odd thing to say about a restaurant.

"Here we are," Michael said. "You can open your eyes now."

My lids slid apart and adjusted to the light. I gazed around, left and right, searching for the café Michael had spent all of this time hiding from me. I couldn't see anything but apartment buildings, staring down from high up. The closest one had the name Stonework Village written on the canopy above the entrance.

I turned to Michael in confusion. "I don't understand? Why are we here? There's no restaurant or café around."

Michael stared at me while a smile crept wider and wider across his face.

"What is this?" I asked.

"Home."

"Home?"

"You heard me right. This is our new home. I've just signed the contracts to purchase an apartment in the building."

My mouth fell open as I tried to respond. I felt nothing but a stab of anger swelling up inside me.

"And not just any apartment, either. I bought us one of the top-floor apartments. You can see parts of Central Park when you're up there."

I shook my head and pushed past the jumbled words in my mouth. "Are you serious? Is this a joke?"

"It's no joke, honey. This is our new home. And the best part is, I got it for five percent under market value. A client of mine works in the building and told me the owner was desperate to sell. Can you believe it?"

I couldn't believe it. We hadn't discussed this at all, and he'd gone and purchased an expensive apartment on the Upper West Side. Even with Michael's income, there was no way we could afford this.

"I don't know where to start," I said. I took a step back from him.

"What do you mean?" he asked. "I thought you'd be happy with a surprise like this."

I scoffed. "There are surprises, and then there are surprises. To begin with, you bought this apartment behind my back without any discussion at all. It's in an area you know I don't want to live in, and it's way out of our price range. I'm not sure how else I'm supposed to react."

"You are supposed to appreciate what I've done for our family."

"Appreciate? All of our money will be sucked into this thing. Aren't you the least bit concerned about that?"

"Not in the slightest. I got a huge promotion at work last week. They've almost doubled my wage. I'm going to be taking on bigger clients."

I slapped my hand over my mouth for a moment, trying to contain my anger. It didn't work. "You didn't think to lead with that? Though it still doesn't change the fact that you didn't discuss this with me first. You promised me months ago that we would pick a place together. You swore to me." I felt my hands begin to clench tight as my nostrils flared.

"I know I did, but…"

He couldn't even finish his sentence.

"You lied to me, straight to my face. This building will forever remind me of that."

Michael shook his head with a smile I only ever saw before he was about to have a serious argument with me. "This is unbelievable. I've worked my ass off the last few months to get this promotion, and all you care about is that I 'lied' to you. People lie to each other every day, honey. I see it all the time in my job: wives lie to save their husbands from jail; parents lie to protect their children from the courtroom. It's just the way things are."

Again, Michael was using the grand wisdom of his job to justify being an asshole. I don't know why he thought this would work.

"I know you work hard, Michael," I said. "No one knows that better than I do, but just because you earn all of the money doesn't mean I don't get a say about where we raise our child. I'm the one growing her inside me. Not you."

"This will be an amazing home for our child. The park is right there, there are incredible schools in the area, and she will have all of Manhattan at her fingertips."

I went to respond, but the words didn't want to come out. I shook my head at him instead. There was no point in explaining how I felt.

We stared at each other, both unwilling to concede our positions. Michael maintained his distance from me as people passed us by, swiveling around the arguing couple.

I rubbed my belly and felt the baby kick me several times. I realized I'd let myself get all worked up over the apartment, and that had put stress upon her. I had to calm myself down immediately. I drew in a deep gulp of air and let it flow out of me. I repeated the process until I felt my heart begin to slow down.

Michael saw me doing this and came to the same conclusion. "I'm sorry for yelling," he said, as he took a few steps toward me. "I wasn't thinking straight. Is she okay?"

I heard his words in my head and tried my hardest not to turn them against him. I wanted to point out that he was only ever worried about the baby, that he didn't care if I got hurt from an argument. I pushed out the fantasy of telling him how I felt with a long exhale. "We're fine," I said.

"Good." Michael removed his gaze from me and started rubbing my arm with his palm. I wanted to shrug him off, but the gentle touch was more than I'd felt from him in a long time.

What happened to us? We used to be a fun couple who couldn't get enough of one another. We were, above all other things, friends. We never let money come between us—we didn't have any to argue over. We never let anger take over. Now, it felt like we were complete strangers, thrown together to have a baby.

Would our relationship survive the first month of her life?

I turned to Michael, not wanting to think about the negative possibilities. "You might as well give me the tour," I said.

"Really?" he asked, as a smile began to form on his lips.

I didn't want to encourage or reward his decision to go behind my back in such a way, but what was done was done. I had no option but to deal with the reality of it all, or take some drastic measures to get myself out of the situation. I was too tired and pregnant to do the latter.

"Let's get one thing clear: I'm nowhere near close to forgiving you. But I guess I don't have a choice now, do I? So let's see what this new home of yours is like."

Michael gave me a nervous chuckle. "That's the spirit, honey," he said, as he guided me to the building. He knew this would happen. He knew I'd have no choice but to accept this place as my new home. I was seven months pregnant and jobless.

Well played, I thought. Little did I know this building would be the end of us.

CHAPTER 19

Now

The paramedics do what they can, but Alan remains unresponsive. They have him laid out on a stretcher with a neck brace on to keep him still. He has gauze wrapped around his skull; blood is seeping through from a wound across his forehead. I think of the red splatter of liquid we found in the stairwell near level four.

According to the paramedics, Alan sustained blunt force trauma consistent with a fall toward a concrete wall. At best, all we can guess is that he tripped down the steps and slammed head first into the hard surface. How he got up to his apartment is the real mystery.

"We found blood on the fourth floor, leading from the stairwell to the elevator," says Henry. "But this doesn't make sense. How did you guys know he was injured and inside his apartment?"

"Alan called us," says the female paramedic.

"Okay," Henry replies, his brow furrowed as he turns to face the woman. "How?"

"A delay in his injuries kicking in. He hit his head hard, but the real damage came later, when his brain began to swell with bruising. He probably called us immediately after it happened and took the elevator up to this apartment. Looks like he managed to get back inside only to collapse on the floor."

My head spins as I think about what this all means. I thought we were following a trail that would point us to Alice, but Alan had been the one bleeding this entire time. I feel relieved that my Bunny hasn't been hurt, but at the same time, she is still out there and missing. Whether she is lost or is in the grip of a kidnapper, I still don't know.

"We'd better get going," the paramedic says. "If you have any suspicions about Alan's injuries, please call the police."

"We've already called the police," I say. "They should be here soon, once the big gas leak downtown clears up."

"Gas leak?" the paramedic asks, as the two push Alan out of the apartment. "I wasn't aware there was one." The EMTs disappear out of the apartment.

I turn to Henry with both hands raised, wanting to know why the paramedics hadn't heard of any gas leak. Maybe these two have just come on duty and don't know about the situation downtown. It seems plausible, until I see Henry's eyes dart left and right.

"Did you call the police?" I ask him. "Is there even a gas leak?"

Henry goes to speak, but his mouth hangs open. No words come out.

"Well?"

"It's too complicated to explain."

"Too complicated? Alice has been taken by someone and you've been lying to me about the police being on their way. How simple is that to explain?"

"You don't know if she has been kidnapped."

My mouth pops open in disgust. "What are you saying, exactly?"

"That there's no proof to suggest anyone came into this building and snatched up your daughter. You thought that blood came from her. It's Alan's."

"I know, but it doesn't change the certainty that she is missing, does it?"

Henry moves over to me and grabs hold of my arms. I cringe at his touch. "My boss told me to avoid calling the police unless absolutely necessary. I was just doing what I was told. Besides, a child could never get out of this building on their own without me knowing about it."

"Screw you! And your employer!" I yell.

"Listen to me for a minute, Erika. What if she's just missing? Maybe no one has taken her. Maybe she's just hiding really well. There's no need to involve the police in that."

"The police could help find her, kidnapper or not. She's been missing for too long. This isn't a game." I stare at Henry and feel an overwhelming sense of rage take over my every thought. How could he be so careless about this situation? Does keeping his job mean more to him than the life of a child?

I stumble away from him with one hand on my head. "I can't tell you why, but I know she has been taken. I can feel it in my heart."

Henry's eyes flick left and right, studying me as his brows furrow with concern. "You can't just go running around accusing people of something only you suspect to be true."

"You don't understand," I say, as I think about Michael. I can't spill anything about him to Henry. Not yet.

"Tell me what it is that I don't understand."

I step past him and pace around the apartment. I grab my hair as I debate what to say to Henry. I close my eyes for a moment. "I can't. You won't believe me. It doesn't matter, anyway. I've wasted too much time. Time that Alice doesn't have." I turn away from him to leave.

"Where are you going?"

I pause, but not to answer Henry's question. I didn't see it when I came in; it was hidden by the open door. Toppled over behind the thick piece of timber is a colorful backpack that looks exactly like Alice's. My hand flies to my mouth as I drop down to the floor. I lean out and grab the bag.

"What are you doing?" Henry asks.

I open the tiny backpack, remembering the day I bought it for Alice. I was visiting a few nearby suburbs close to where Alice and I lived, trying to get a head start on which elementary school to send her to. We dropped in to my favorite school of the three we planned on visiting that day. We hadn't made it past the front of reception when Alice saw a colorful bag the school had on sale. It was sold for the kindergarten associated with the academy.

Alice begged me to buy it. I'll never forget the way her eyes lit up when I handed it over to her.

"Thank you, Mommy," she said, dozens of times that day. I'd never seen her love an object like that, except for her copy of *Alice's Adventures in Wonderland.*

"Whose bag is that?" Henry asked, pulling me back to the present.

I swiveled around and stared into his eyes, fighting back the tears. "It's Alice's." I open the zip of the central section and start searching inside. Every item has been taken out. I curse myself for not penning Alice's name into the bag in case it ever went missing.

Henry's mouth drops open as his eyes double in size. "What the hell? Why has Alan got Alice's backpack?"

"That's what I want to know," I say. The question needs an answer. I get up from the floor and hurry back to Henry. I place the bag down on Alan's counter and move up to the receptionist, breaching his personal space.

"Do you see what I'm saying now? Someone has taken Alice. Alan knows who."

Henry closes his eyes, as if he is trying to think. "I don't know. Maybe Alan found the bag before he fell over."

"And carried it all the way back here?"

Henry takes a step back and scratches at his skull. "It might already have been on his shoulder. Maybe he didn't realize it was still on him when he dragged himself to his apartment?"

"That's a big maybe."

I shake my head at him as I start pacing around the apartment. There's got to be more here. Something that implicates Alan or Desmond. Maybe Desmond stored the bag in Alan's apartment without the old man knowing. But I can't ask Alan directly. Considering the head injury he sustained, Alan will be lucky to be alive after today.

"What are you doing now?" Henry groans.

"Looking for something else to show you what I mean. There has to be another piece of evidence in this apartment to show you I'm right about my suspicions."

Henry stomps over to me and gets in my way. "Tell me what your suspicions are. I want to hear you say them out loud."

I stop moving and let out a huff of air. "Alan may or may not be involved in Alice's disappearance."

"How? Just because of a backpack?"

"Not just that. There's also Desmond."

"Desmond? Who is that?"

I frown. "I thought it was your job to know everyone who lived or worked here?"

"I don't, sorry. Like I said, I've only been here for a month. I'm still learning names and the way things are done."

I stare at him. "So you don't know, do you?"

"Know what?" he asks, crossing his arms.

I debate telling him. Is this information worth more to me as a secret? I don't know anymore, so I come right out and say it. "The man in apartment 707—the criminal. His name is Desmond Bracero."

"Bracero?" Henry asks.

I see something ticking around in his brain; he's trying to work out what I'm getting at. The light bulb goes off, and his eyes go wide. "Wait, what?"

"Alan is Desmond's father. He got him a job in maintenance here. He got him into the building, into apartment 707, despite his criminal past."

Henry tries to rebut my claim, but he fails to come up with any words. He shakes his head at me, his eyes filled with anguish. The truth hits him hard.

"This is beyond crazy," Henry says. "I mean, I knew that guy worked and lived in the building. I didn't know he was Alan's son, though."

"He is. And I've been told he has a criminal history. And now Alice's backpack is here in his father's apartment."

Henry holds up a hand to me, trying to fend off my words. He wants all of his problems to go away at once. "What are you getting at?"

"Desmond," I say.

"What about him?"

"He must have Alice. I believe he and his father worked together to kidnap her."

"That's a lot of guessing there. How do you know Desmond has Alice?"

"He has to. How else is she still missing? Why is my Bunny's backpack here?"

I rush around the apartment and start tearing it apart, pulling items off shelves, swiping papers around, looking under pillows. There's still the final piece of the puzzle to show to Henry, and it involves the one name I'm yet to bring up: Michael. I can't connect Alan and Desmond to my ex-husband yet, but I will. Michael thinks he has made himself invincible by paying others to do his dirty work, but he is far from safe.

"Stop it!" Henry yells. "You're making a mess of Alan's apartment."

"Either help me look or leave. You didn't call the police when you said you had. You owe me."

Henry shakes his head at me. "I don't even know what you're looking for. This has gone on long enough. I'm putting a stop to this shit right now." He grabs hold of my arm and pulls me away from a stack of papers on a small table in the living area. They all fall to the floor and spread out. Henry continues to pull me back and away from the chaos.

"Let me go," I yell. "I need to find something to point me toward Alice."

"There's nothing here, dammit." He gets a good hold of my arms and yanks me away.

"Wait," I say, freezing in place. I stare down at a single business card as it slides across the floor before me. It's newer than the one I have in my handbag, but the name and contact info are still the same. "Pick up that business card," I tell Henry.

"What?" he says. He maintains his grip on me but eases up, sensing my lack of resistance. He reaches out with his left hand and grabs the card from the floor. He holds it up to read it aloud. "Michael Walls. Attorney at law."

I feel his grip release as his mouth falls open. He places both hands on the business card and mutters to himself over and over.

I brush myself off and stand back. Henry keeps his focus on the card. "What does this mean?"

"Alan has Michael's business card. And he has Alice's backpack in his apartment."

"Why?" is all Henry can ask me.

CHAPTER 20

Henry stares at Michael's business card. "Your ex is a criminal lawyer. Maybe he knew that and gave Alan the card in case his son ever needed it. And maybe the backpack just looks like Alice's."

I shake my head at Henry as we stand in Alan's apartment, surrounded by the mess I've made. I leave Michael out of the conversation for the moment. "What business does Alan have with a small child's backpack?"

"Like I said, maybe he found it and decided to keep it to hand in."

"It's hers. I know it is." I try to keep my voice level as I curse myself again for not writing Alice's name inside the backpack. I always thought people that did that were being overly cautious. I figured I could always buy her a new one if it went missing or got stolen.

Henry paces around Alan's apartment, eyes on the floor as he clutches Michael's card. Thoughts and ideas are rattling around in his brain, and I can see he wants to unload them on me. I don't like where this conversation is heading. I need to steer him back on course.

I grab his arm gently. "Henry, please. I promise you that is Alice's bag. I came here today with her to see Michael. He should have been here, but he's nowhere to be found. Instead, there's an ex-con across the hall whose father has had a major fall. He's also nowhere to be seen. Doesn't that sound odd to you?"

"Maybe he doesn't know about his father yet."

"Or maybe he's staying inside where he is safe. My daughter went missing on this floor—a floor that has two maintenance workers on it with the know-how to rig an elevator to screw up at the right moment. Alan was in the lobby when I went up, and Desmond was on this level. That has to mean something, right?"

Henry stares into my eyes, his brow tight. He is torn between two possibilities. I have to convince him of the truth. He can't abandon me now.

"And what about Michael?" he asks me.

I know I have to tread lightly. My next words could make or break my argument. "What do you think about Michael?" I ask, not trying to influence his thinking until I know where he's at.

"I don't know. I guess it's weird that his card is here. If Alan and Desmond have anything to do with Alice going missing, it seems a bit too convenient that Michael isn't home during a time when you were expecting him to be."

"Exactly," I say, a big grin across my face. "God, it pains me to think it, but I know Michael has done something. Something awful."

"How do you know, though? What sort of person is your ex-husband?"

It's a loaded question, one that can't be answered in a few sentences, but I have to try. "When Alice was only six months old, we got a divorce. Six months old. He left me to handle her every problem like it was my responsibility and no one else's."

Henry shakes his head at me. Disgust wrinkles his forehead. I absorb the disdain he must feel toward Michael and know it is only going to get worse.

Michael forced us apart so soon after what happened; I can still barely handle thinking about it. That day wasn't my fault. I never wanted things to go that way, but they did. I shake off the memory and got back to what needs to be said.

"After I came to accept that he was incapable of being there for us, I made sure the court knew he deserved to see Alice as little as possible. Despite his contacts and an army of lawyers, I sued him for full custody and won. He got weekend visitations set to one afternoon per two-week period. He did not take that well. To be honest, neither did I. Sure, it was good getting his beloved money to help pay for Alice, but those few poisonous hours he spent with her were more than I wanted my Bunny to be exposed to. I wanted him gone from our lives."

Henry doesn't say a word. He just listens. He's only young and doesn't understand what damage a determined person can do when push comes to shove. Maybe he had a good family or grew up with someone normal, but soon enough, he would see what families were capable of.

"Ever since," I continue, "he's treated his daughter like a possession to be reclaimed in small doses. He's made subtle threats to take her away. I know that he is trying to show the system that I'm not fit to be a mother. I have to bust my ass every single day to prove I am a good mother, just to keep him at bay. I never thought he would take things to the next level, though."

"The next level?"

"You know exactly what I mean."

Henry keeps his eyes away from me, not wanting to hear the truth. "Don't say it," he mutters.

"I have to. Someone does."

Henry focuses on me with all of his attention. I can see the realization brewing inside him. He sees it all coming together into one screwed-up piece.

"You think Michael arranged for Alan and Desmond to kidnap your daughter."

The words fall out of his mouth and fill me with relief and dread at the same time. "I don't just think it; I know it."

"God," Henry says, both hands twisted into his hair. "This can't be happening."

"I don't want it to be the truth either. Any other possibility would be better, but here we are."

Henry lets out a long sigh, both eyes squeezed shut. I feel my wrist begin to shake again, and try to steady my trembling arm before I lose control, hoping he doesn't notice. He opens his eyes back up and returns his focus to me. We stare at each other as a heavy silence fills the air.

"What do we do now?" he asks, finally.

I turn around and look toward the door. "He could be across the hall."

"Desmond?"

"Yes. And if he is, I'll need your help to confront him."

Henry grabs my upper arms again. "If he's in there with your little girl, I guarantee he'll be armed. We should call the police and wait for them to arrive. In fact, I'm calling them right now." He pulls out his smartphone and dials 911, placing the call on loudspeaker a second later.

I shake my head, still furious he never actually called the authorities to begin with, but I have no choice but to cooperate with Henry. "I'm not waiting for anyone. Either you help me, or I go to him by myself."

The receptionist from Stonework Village stares into my eyes as he faces the most challenging question he's probably ever been asked.

"Hello, 911, what is your emergency?" a voice says over the speaker.

I walk to the door, not willing to wait for an answer that might never come.

"Erika," Henry calls to me, as I reach the door.

I spin on the spot and face him, waiting for the next words out of his mouth.

CHAPTER 21

Henry disconnects the call to the police, a faltering expression in his eyes. He is going to try and talk me out of confronting Desmond. I squeeze my fists tight knowing that he still hasn't called the police, but I can't let him stop me from leaving. I need to show Henry that I am not afraid to die to get Alice back from Desmond, or Michael, or anyone else stupid enough to take my daughter away.

"Say it," I blurt out. "I know what you're thinking."

"I can't let you do this. It's too dangerous."

I grip the doorframe, ready to bolt. Henry is a few paces away. I could get a head start and reach Desmond's door before him. Unfortunately, he'd be right behind me and able to pull me away from the situation, giving Desmond enough time to run off with Alice out the fire escape.

"I'm not scared of him," I say.

"You should be. If he's what you say he is, then you could be putting yourself in danger. Is that what you want?"

I let a slither of silence edge its way into our conversation as I try to think of a solution. Henry is only trying to stop me from getting hurt for the sake of his job. He doesn't really care about me. I need to do this. I have to.

"It's not what I want, but I'm ready to do what it takes to save her. Alice's life is worth more than mine. It always has been. It always will be."

Henry takes a small shuffle toward me. I pull on the doorframe and step partially out of the apartment. Did he think I wouldn't notice his less-than-subtle approach?

"What do you think you're doing, Henry? I won't let you stop me. Just stay out of my way."

He holds up a palm toward me. "I'm not trying to stop you, okay? Just let me through first, so I can help you."

He's lying. I can detect it across his brow—a slight twitch. He's planning on grabbing me the second he can, so I don't run out the door toward Desmond. I decide to play his game and see where he is going with it.

"Okay. I'll let you through." I glance down the hallway for a quick second. We both know apartment 707 is down to the right from here. I step out into the corridor. "I'll even move out of your way."

"Don't do it," he says. "It'll only take me a second to catch up."

"I know it will," I whisper.

Henry sees the pause in my step and knows I'm about to charge. What he doesn't realize is my pivot is in the opposite direction. I run away, moving left instead of right, to the end of the corridor.

"Wait," Henry calls out.

I peek over my shoulder and hear his footfalls behind. He's taken the bait. I focus forward and dig deep, running through the mostly empty floor in an attempt to confuse Henry so I can confront Desmond on my own. I don't need anyone else to help me. Not even the police. No one ever comes to my aid when I need them. Why should that change now?

Henry's calls become muffled by the thick carpeting and walls of the corridors as I move around the corner and charge through the seventh floor. I'm losing him with ease as I sprint faster and faster away in the limited space despite the pain in my legs. Henry thought he could control me the way Michael used to, trying to convince me I didn't have a say in the choices I made.

One of Michael's most recent afternoons with Alice sits in the forefront of my mind as I stop and hide behind a support column. I think back to that day and how important it is now.

I met up with Michael at a café not far from his apartment. It was Michael's day with Alice, so we completed the handover in a public place where no one could cause a scene. Or at least, a scene not as bad as it could be. The situation had such a tremendous potential for failure that we insisted upon a mediator being present in the café, waiting at a close distance, to keep things civil.

Michael only had his daughter for six hours every second Sunday, as agreed with the judge, but it felt like twice as long. I rarely ever brought Alice directly to his apartment. The building sent a shudder down my spine that could not be explained. Maybe it was the thought of it being the place where our relationship died.

As always, we sent Alice off to the corner of the café reserved for small children to play in. There was a short table with pencil markings all over it and a handful of half-broken toys. Alice sat down in a chair, her copy of *Alice's Adventures in Wonderland* out already set on the table. She flicked through the book and read out loud the sections she could recall by memory alone, blissfully unaware that her parents were about to have another argument.

"Why do we do this here?" Michael asked the mediator. "Surely there are other places more suited."

"No, this is perfect," I said, grabbing his attention. "You can't yell out loud in this tiny space and ignore other people."

"What do you mean? I don't yell."

I scoffed. "Right, so you've never publicly humiliated me just to get your point across? I didn't realize. That must have all been in my mind."

He shook his head. "Don't talk to me like that, Erika. I am being perfectly civil and not trying to—"

I held up my hand. "Look, I'm not here for an argument. I'm here to get this pointless task over with so I can go about my life without these constant interruptions."

"Interruptions? You can't be serious? I—"

I stopped him again before his voice got louder than what was acceptable for a café. I could see it taking all of his self-control, but he bit his tongue to prevent further outrage.

"Fine. Have it your way," Michael said. "Call this whatever you want to call it. I know the truth."

"The truth? Please." I turned away to my Bunny before I got into another fight with Michael. I watched her sweet eyes flicker over every word as her finger traced each line of text in her book. How could someone with such a beautiful soul come from two such flawed people?

I turned back to Michael. "I'm sorry for my comments. That's not why we're here. I have to remember that."

"You know exactly why we're here. You can't avoid this, Erika."

I grip my coffee cup a little tighter. "I know I can't avoid this. I'm not trying to. I'm just saying I'm sorry, is all."

Michael didn't say a word or offer his own regret. He couldn't handle apologizing to a person, even if it meant steering the conversation in the right direction.

I moved on. "I'm here today because I feel like this arrangement is no longer working."

"No longer working? What do you mean?" he asked.

I huffed out my breath. I needed to be honest with him. "I mean this entire situation is nothing but a toxic experience for all of us. It needs to come to an end."

Michael shook his head more than half a dozen times. "No. You don't get to decide that. It's out of your hands."

"I know it is, but if you agree to do what is best and contact the court, we could all save ourselves the trouble and move on. We could do what's best for Bunny." I waved a hand toward Alice.

Michael twisted his brows and turned to study his little girl. He closed his eyes and dropped his head. He turned back to me and filled his lungs with anger. I could tell at that moment that the public space was not going to stop what was about to spew out of his mouth.

"You can't keep doing this."

"No," I said, louder than I wanted to. "You don't belong in her life. You never did. I want you out of it. Why should she have six hours of every second Sunday ruined so you can feel like a father?" I was standing at this point. It took me a moment to realize, but everyone was staring, Alice included.

I sat back down and held my face in my palms, silently cursing myself for being the one to upset the peace. I slowly lifted my head back up to see Michael gawking at me like the rest of them.

"Are you done?" he asked.

"Am I done? I'll never be done, you understand?" I kept my voice low enough for the patrons of the café to go back to their overpriced beverages.

"I understand, Erika. I understand all too well. But you know what? I'm done. I thought I could handle this mess for the rest of my life, but clearly I can't." He stood from the table in a rush, knocking over his half-filled black coffee.

"What does that mean? Are you going to leave us alone?"

Michael's eyes flicked to mine, his lowered brow almost stabbing into the bridge of his nose. "You'd like that, wouldn't you?"

"Yes."

"Well, Erika, life's not that simple. Sometimes you have to accept the truth. I know things will never change between us. We've had this conversation a thousand times before. But maybe it's time I finally made a change of my own."

"What are you on about?"

Michael dusted himself off for a moment before he nodded at the mediator. "Enjoy the rest of your day." Without another word, he left the café, cutting through the cramped room, leaving his daughter behind like a forgotten piece of luggage. He didn't stop to look back or change his mind.

"Where's he going?" the mediator asked me, hurrying over to the table.

I couldn't answer her question. I didn't know.

I've thought about that moment for the last month. Michael's thinly veiled threat scared me enough to think about taking Alice away from him. I should have done something sooner, though. I waited too long to finally act. I shake my head as I remain hidden behind the support column.

"Erika," I hear Henry call out. His yell brings me back to the present. I am still catching my breath as I hide from the receptionist who thinks he is doing me a favor.

I glimpse back to see him confused and lost at the other end of the corridor. From here, all I need to do is backtrack while Henry is distracted, and then go to Desmond's apartment. Henry will be too far away to stop me.

I force myself to move quietly over the carpet. My feet press lightly against the surface, yet they ache from going up and down the stairwell. Every step I take, no matter how light or heavy, sends small shock waves up through my body that will do their damage over the next few days. I don't care, though. My body isn't the priority. It's Alice, my little girl, whom I have failed to protect from harm.

I reach the middle corridor and start to run. Desmond's apartment is so close I can see the numbers. Henry rushes out from behind and grips me with both hands to slow me down.

"No!" I yell, as he moves in front of me to block my path to 707. "You can't. I need to save her. She's in there."

"We don't know that, Erika. It's not safe."

A few of the residents come out of their apartments, to see what all the fuss is about. They are stepping out from behind doors I had previously knocked on. One remains shut: 707.

"Look what you've done," I say to Henry. "He'll know now. He'll know we're on to him."

Henry doesn't answer. He instead focuses all of his energy on blocking me. I try to push by him, but he easily stops my weakened body.

"Just calm down, Erika. I'm going to call the police. They will be here soon."

"I don't need them here to—"

The elevator opens with a ding, pulling both of us toward it. Desmond steps out and sees us near his door. He has a plastic bag in his hand. He sees me watching him as he steps back slightly. He thinks we've called the police. Then, time slows down.

Alice takes a single step out of the elevator. Desmond drops the bag and scoops her up in his arms and launches himself back into the elevator. The items smash down with a thud and break. Glass shatters and liquids spray in all directions. I instantly smell alcohol in the air.

I rush away from Henry toward Desmond. The elevator doors roll shut with a thud before I take two steps. "No," I yell, as I run for the call button. I reach out, but it's too far away. I won't be able to stop the elevator from going to its next destination, whether it be up or down.

I hit the button and repeat the motion over and over, as if the twentieth time will magically pry the doors open.

Henry grabs my hand and stops me from hitting the button. He stares into my eyes, knowing that he has potentially sealed Alice's fate. "I'm sorry."

"Up or down?" I say in reply, as I think about Alice having to travel up and down the building inside an elevator. "Tell me which way they went."

CHAPTER 22

Then

Being patient had never been my strong suit. I'd always been the type to want things to happen in a timely, efficient manner. The research I did in Brooklyn Heights turned out to be a waste of time when Michael purchased the apartment on the Upper West Side, and it forced me to rethink our future in its entirety.

I had been living in the new apartment for a few weeks now and was eight and a half months along with my pregnancy with Alice. I was sitting in our local Starbucks, waiting to meet Michael, when I received a call from his cell.

"What is it this time?" I asked him, knowing he was going to cancel our lunch date again.

"I'm sorry, honey," he said. "One of our big clients needs an extra meeting to go over something important. I'm going to be about twenty minutes late. I'd get out of it if I could, but they—"

"I don't want to hear it," I said. "I've heard every possible excuse now. There's nothing you can say that I will believe. Just admit that you don't want—"

"It's not like that and you know it. God, I'm so sick of this. I'm out here busting my ass for our family, so our child has everything she will ever need and so you don't ever have to work another day in your life, and this is the attitude I get in return."

I allowed a wall of silence to form between us. I decided not to give him any more ammunition for his pathetic, selfish argument.

"Say something," he said.

"What's the point? I don't have anything left to say to you. If you can't understand why it's important to keep your promises after all this time, then I guess you never will."

I heard a massive sigh roll down the line and out of my cell. I could picture Michael fuming and about to explode on the other end. If I weren't so heavily pregnant, I was sure he would have totally lost his cool and really let me have it.

"I have to go," he said.

"Don't let me keep you. I'll see you at home." I stamped my finger on the screen, ending the call to let Michael know I wouldn't be waiting the twenty minutes. I'd done it before and ended up sitting around for more than an hour waiting for him to grace me with his presence. I tossed the device down on the table with a clatter.

"Erika," shouted out one of the baristas, holding up my decaf coffee. I knew I shouldn't be drinking it, but things had been so stressful between Michael and I that I found myself ordering one every other day.

The barista saw my swollen belly and brought the beverage to my table. I had ordered the drink to go, knowing in my heart that Michael would cancel. I was getting sick of telling the staff that I would be ordering for another person who was on their way, only to get up and leave after a short time.

I put the coffee away quicker than I should have and decided to head home to the apartment to take a bath. I needed to unwind after the phone call with Michael. I wasn't going to let his crap fall through me to our baby.

Our baby. The statement sounded wrong in my head whenever I said it. Michael had spent most of the pregnancy "working for our future child," as he would put it. He went to as many doctors' appointments as his schedule allowed, eager to find out how the baby was doing. It was never to support me. He went to my pregnancy classes when he had time, but only to ensure I was doing them right.

He thought he was being helpful, but he never once massaged my feet at the end of a long day or cared to find out how I was coping. He just paid for it all and monitored my every move like I was too stupid to work things out on my own.

Michael seemed so proud to be the breadwinner of the family, but there was more to being a father than making a lot of money. It wasn't like he had zero choice in the matter and needed to make ends meet so we could get through it all. He just wanted to keep his career on track and not let something as inconvenient as a pregnancy slow him down.

I made my way the few blocks home and reached the lobby, where I said hello to the receptionist on duty. You could simply walk into the building without swiping your key card first. I shuffled over and into the elevator. As the double doors sealed shut, an overwhelming panic swept in through every crack in the box, as if the elevator were filling with water. The fear seeped in and made its way to the corners of my brain I thought were safe from harm.

I thought about Michael and our future. Would we make it with a baby in our lives? Would that be too much for our fragile marriage to handle? It would all be my fault if things failed. The voice in the back of my head told me so whenever things went wrong.

I pulled the stop button and fell to my knees.

CHAPTER 23

Now

Henry stares at me with his mouth open and both hands scrunching up his hair.

"Which way did they go?" I ask him again, as I stand by the elevator that has whisked Desmond and Alice out of my grasp. "Up or down?"

"It sounded like it went up," he says.

"Are you sure?"

He stares up at the elevator doors and thinks about his answer for a second longer than I feel comfortable with. "Pretty sure."

His words hit me hard. I need more confidence than that from him. I feel my stomach twist into knots at the thought of being so close to finding Alice. She was right there, only a few strides away, but I couldn't get to her in time to save her from Desmond—all because of Henry.

"I'm going to need more than 'pretty sure'!" I yell. The residents who had come to see what all the fuss was about have left and gone back into their apartments. Only an old woman remains, staring at me for a moment too long before she shuffles back inside.

"There's no external display telling us where the elevator is coming from. It just appears when it's available. But I could hear the car going up."

I shake my head as the seconds tick away. I move toward the stairs, knowing I need to go either up or down. Which way would Desmond take her? Would he go to the ground, deciding to flee the building, or would he take her to a hiding place somewhere inside Stonework Village?

I try to think what Michael would have planned on doing. He'd have Alice kept nearby. The closer the better. He'd want the control of being able to have her safely produced at any moment so he could find her. He could show everyone and a judge that I was an unfit parent who lost her child, and have Alice finally taken out of my hands.

"I don't know what else to tell you," Henry says.

I walk away from him for a moment, trying to clear my head. Henry stays near the elevator and leans on its frame. Just as I'm about to lose my cool, I see Henry's security key card on the ground where we had wrestled. I glance over my shoulder as I walk to it. He's still staring at the elevator, so I scoop it into my hand and shove it into my pocket. By the time he realizes it's missing, I'll be long gone.

"I'm going up," I say.

"Okay," Henry replies. "I'll head to the lobby to cut him off if he goes back down. I can lock down the building with my phone from here. I'm calling the police, too, while I'm at it."

I don't respond as I run through the entry to the stairwell and begin my climb. Henry has to know how mad I am that he held me back and allowed Desmond to slip away. But he also knows that I still need him to handle things until the police arrive.

I pull myself up the steps as quickly as possible. I decide to go up the stairs to pursue Desmond, figuring he must be taking Alice back to where he has been hiding her. That place has to be near Michael. Maybe I interrupted Desmond going back to his apartment, or Alan's, for something he needed so badly he was willing to risk being caught out in the open with Alice.

What did he need? Was it something for my Bunny, something vital? I try to push the thought out of my head that some ex-con is responsible for my daughter's welfare during her kidnapping.

I'm running for the fourteenth floor, but I decide I'll stop at each level in between to do a quick sweep. All the while, I can't help but think Desmond could have gone in the opposite direction, heading for the lobby to escape with my daughter out into the busy city streets. The thought sends a shooting fear down my spine that causes me to stumble and misplace my step. How good is Henry's ability to lock down the building against someone who works in maintenance?

I fall up into the stairwell, slamming my head into a wall. I feel a sting of pain that is quickly followed by a warm sensation. I scramble to my feet and keep going to open the door to the eighth floor. I don't have time to waste checking if I'm okay, despite the pain in my head. Desmond could be close, and I'm not letting him get away. No one takes my daughter from me. No one. I don't care if Michael makes me look like the worst parent in the world, I will fight until my last breath to get Alice back.

I run through the eighth floor, finding it to be almost identical to the one below. A few of the residents are moving about their day without a care in the world. They have no idea what disturbing things have been going on in their building. I rush up to the first person I see.

"Have you seen a little girl come through here with a bald man?"

The middle-aged woman, dressed in sportswear, moves a step back from me and shakes her head. "No, sorry."

I probably look deranged to her—at best—but I had to ask. "If you see anything, call reception straight away."

She brushes by me in a hurry and says no more. I spot a man in a suit leaving his apartment. I rush toward him with intent. He sees my eyes focusing in on his, and backs up with a defensive posture.

"What do you want?" he asks preemptively.

"Have you seen a little girl come through here?"

"No. I've been in my apartment all morning." The man doesn't look at me as he continues on down the corridor to the elevator, adjusting his tie as he goes.

I continue on, knowing these residents are useless and uncaring at best. Why are people so unwilling to help each other? Why don't we trust anyone we meet? As I run around the floor, searching in desperation for Desmond and Alice, I can't help but think back to the first time I took her to playgroup. The judgmental eyes of those parents will stay with me forever.

My mind falls back a year to the moment I walked up to the entrance of the playgroup building, Alice's hand tightly in mine as she shuffled along by my side. It was her first half-day visit, with six other children around the same age, to the small play center that was close to my apartment.

"Mommy, please," Alice said, while resisting me enough to slow my stride. I decided to step her off to the side to see what all the fuss was about. She gazed up at me with doleful eyes.

"It's going to be okay, Bunny."

"No, it won't, Mommy. They won't like me."

"What do you mean?" I asked, as I squatted down to her level and brushed some hair away from her face. "They'll love you."

Her eyes darted around. She stared at the building and glanced back at me before shaking her head. "That's not what Daddy says."

I let out a puff of frustration. I wanted to shout and demand what the hell Michael had been saying to Alice to make her think such a thing, but I held my tongue as best I could.

"What did Daddy say to you?"

Alice fiddled with her hands and shifted her focus to the ground. "He said that as soon as the other mommies meet you, they won't like me and neither will their kids."

"What the he—" I stopped myself from cussing in front of Alice. She didn't deserve to be worried about something

Michael had said to insult me. I shook my head and closed my eyes for a moment to block out his negativity. I needed to be the bigger parent.

"Why won't the other mommies like you?" she asked me.

How could I answer that question? I was beyond pissed that Michael would stoop so low as to try and poison Alice with such a remark. Why was divorce such a messy affair? Even after years of it, he still found the time to get little jabs in.

"Mommy?"

"They will like me, Bunny. And, you know what, even if they don't, I'm still going to be nice to them. Do you know why?"

She shook her head.

"Because we're better than that. We don't say things that aren't nice to other people. If they did that to us, it would upset us and make us feel bad."

"Okay, Mommy," she said with a cheesy grin. "I'll be nice, and they'll be nice."

"Exactly. Couldn't have put it better myself. Now let's head inside and make some friends."

"Okay," Alice said in her high-pitched bubbly voice. She held up her hand for me to grab hold. I wrapped my fingers around hers and continued to walk along the path toward the playgroup entrance. We pushed through the heavy door and saw the other families had already arrived. Chatty mothers and busy children filled the small room. It was clear that they knew one another.

Alice stayed still, matching my frozen state. I didn't know what to do or what to say to blend in with them. I felt like the new kid in school, the one nobody wanted to talk to out of fear of being ostracized. A momentary hush washed over the space as a few of the moms stared at me. I swore I saw sneers forming on their lips.

"Come on, Bunny," I heard myself say, as I moved Alice along toward the rest of the pack. The stares of the other parents hit me, making me feel as though I could never be trusted. Michael's words spun around in my head. The mothers continued to go about their conversations in lowered voices. Only now, I was positive I was the topic of their discussions.

I decided to not let anyone bother me, and encouraged Alice to join in the fun with the other children, who were already playing.

Michael was somehow right. They didn't like me the second they met me. But that didn't seem to fit the looks on their faces. It wasn't that they didn't like me; it was as if Michael had called ahead and told them all that I couldn't be trusted. I knew that wasn't the case, but it was hard not to let my mind think such stupid thoughts.

Knowing I needed to set the tone for Alice, I refused to let the other children judge my Bunny in the same way. Fortunately, they allowed her to play. The innocence of a child took more than a few judgmental parents to defeat.

Alice melded into the group within minutes while I sat on the outside of the inner circle of the playgroup, feeling about as pathetic as a person could.

After ten minutes of Alice enjoying her time, I took a few steps away from the room and pulled out my cell. I dialed Michael's number and sighed when the call went to voice mail. He wasn't going to get off that easy, so I left him a message. "I know what you said to Alice about playgroup. If you ever try to poison her against me like this again, so help me..." I took a deep breath and hung up. I knew better than to leave threatening messages on his cell, but I couldn't help myself.

I turned back and watched Alice playing without a care in the world. I wondered at what point in our lives we became so scared or fearful of other people that we wouldn't help out a desperate mother trying to do what was right by her daughter.

CHAPTER 24

I search every level above the seventh floor until I reach the top of the stairwell. No one has seen Desmond and Alice, and they don't want to know about it.

I reach fourteen and bust through the door. I look left and right, but no one is around. I charge down the hallway and back again.

I try to determine where they have gone and see 1402 nearby. Surely Desmond wasn't going to Michael's apartment? That would be the dumbest thing he could do right now. Then again, maybe he wasn't a brilliant criminal. It would explain why he had spent time in jail.

I pull out the key card I stole from Henry, unable to rule out the possibility that Alice is close by in her father's apartment with a moronic kidnapper. I raise the master card toward the receiver each apartment has to keep the doors electromagnetically locked. Then something catches my eye.

I turn my head down the wide but short corridor and see a child at the end who wasn't there a moment ago. She's a young girl, around Alice's age, watching me from behind a support column against the wall. She is half hidden from me; I can only see one eye out, and her long hair partially covers her face.

I smile and wave at her as I pocket the key card. She sees my friendly gesture and gives me a toothy grin in return, with a small wave of her own. She comes out from behind her protective space and continues to stare at me.

The little girl cautiously takes a few steps toward me, both hands squeezing the small doll that she is holding in front of her. I think about the doll I stupidly came to this building for. I should have taken Alice away instead of coming here for it. She would have eventually gotten over losing the toy.

The little girl continues to stare. "Hello," I call out to her. I take a few steps in her direction, hoping to ask if she saw anyone come by here.

The little girl giggles for a moment. "Hi," she says. "Can I ask you a question?"

I keep walking toward her, confident she won't run off screaming. "Of course. But I'd also like to ask you a question, too, if that's okay?"

She contemplates what I just said by drumming her fingers on her chin in the most exaggerated, child-like fashion. "Mmm, okay," she says.

"What's your question?" I ask her.

The girl goes a little shy for a few seconds and presses her chin toward her chest, looking sheepish. She giggles again to herself, as if the question is rolling around in her head.

I drop down into a squat in front of the girl and ask her again. "What's your question, honey?"

"Are you a mommy?"

"Yes, I am. How could you tell?"

The little girl giggles again. "Because you look like a mommy."

I don't know what to think of her observation. Should I be offended or flattered? Either way, I encourage her curiosity. "That's very clever of you to work out."

"It was hard. Usually, mommies have their children with them, but I could tell."

I need to ask the girl if she's seen Alice, or if she's noticed anything unusual during her keen moments of observation. "My turn to ask a question. Have you seen a little girl come through here with a bald man? She's about your age."

She shakes her head at me after a few moments of thought. "Sorry."

"That's okay," I say, as my head sinks lower to the ground.

"Jessica?" a voice calls over to us from one of the apartments doorways. I turn to see a man in his early forties looking at me.

"I'm sorry. Is she bothering you?"

"No, not at all."

"Come on, Jessica. We have to get going." The man closes up his apartment and starts moving for the elevator. Jessica follows immediately. "Bye," she says to me, like we'll catch up another time.

"Bye," I whisper. I see the man going and realize he might have seen something. "Before you go, have you seen a little girl and a bald man come through here?"

The man doesn't stop. "No, sorry."

"That's okay," I mutter, as I walk back toward Michael's apartment. The elevator opens. A moment later, the steel doors roll shut, and they are gone, as if they were never here.

I turn to 1402 and let out a long sigh. I always taught Alice not to speak to strangers the way that little girl so confidently did. Look where my great parenting has gotten Alice, though.

I pull the key card from my pocket and raise it up to the door again. I swipe the card faster than the reader can handle and wait for the electromagnetic lock to disengage. The red light turns green, allowing me access.

I push the door open and charge in, not wanting to waste another second.

CHAPTER 25

Desmond could be waiting with a lead pipe, ready to strike me down the second I run inside Michael's apartment. I don't care. He can kill me if he feels the need; it's the only thing that will stop me from finding Alice. She is more valuable to me than my own life could ever be.

I rush inside and quickly see that the first part of the apartment is empty. I stumble out from its grand entryway to a vast open-plan kitchen, dining, and living space, with a step up to a lounge area. Windows grant beautiful views of the city in multiple directions.

I search every bedroom, every area of the apartment, calling out Alice's name every few seconds. They're not here. Have I wasted more time I don't have by rushing headfirst in here like a complete moron? It was so obvious Desmond wouldn't go into Michael's apartment, so why did I do it? Have I sealed Alice's fate with yet another stupid decision?

My hands begin to shake as I spin around on the spot, trying to find the answers to the endless flow of questions that are assaulting my brain. A dark storm is overtaking my every thought as I feel the panic set in and grip me around the throat. I can't breathe, my chest is closing in on itself, and I feel so dizzy I start to stumble.

I grip my forehead to center myself, but once more I feel the sharp pain I tried to ignore in the stairwell. I pull my hand back, but there's no blood on my hand. The thought of the vital fluid, however, intertwines with flashes of Alice's face, making me miss my footsteps as I back up in the central living area of Michael's apartment. I trip and fall.

As I lie on the hard, wooden floorboards and stare at the ceiling, Alice takes over my every thought. Her soft face drowns out the pain and suffering and takes me to another world, where nothing can hurt either one of us.

I stare at her as if she is right in front of me. Her blue eyes gaze back into mine, unblinking. "Alice," I say, as I reach out to a body that isn't there. "Come back to me."

Her eyes close for a long time. When they open, I see the same blue eyes narrowing in on me with an intensity that could only belong to Michael. His face replaces Alice's, drowning out any beauty, swapping it for contempt and loathing.

I can't look away from the man who would do anything to see me lose the child we were supposed to raise together. The sneer on his lips crushes any hope I have of finding Alice and saving her from his sick plans.

I know deep down how things reached this point. I only wish I'd tried harder to stop it. But what could have I done to prevent Michael from kidnapping Alice? That wasn't a question I ever thought I'd be asking myself.

I think back to Michael's warning at the café. He was spelling it out as clear as day. He was about to do something to remove Alice from my life. I should have taken him seriously and made arrangements sooner than later. Instead, I took too long—as usual. I let my incompetence and disorganized state get in the way. Coming here today to retrieve Alice's doll was a huge mistake.

I stare up at the ceiling and realize I need to get off the ground before I let fatigue claim me. My heart leaps out of my chest as I shoot up and climb to my feet. I rub my eyes and wonder how long I would have slept if I'd let it claim me.

I let out a lungful of panicked air and hold my head for a moment with both hands. How could I even contemplate sleep at a time like this? Alice is out there with Desmond while I'm in here taking a break.

I stumble around the apartment to perform a quick search for evidence of Alice's abduction. I need to try and find something while I'm here—clues that might implicate Michael or tell me where Alice is being kept. I might not get another chance.

I rummage through the belongings Michael has tucked away in one of his spare rooms. The apartment is designed for a family with two to three kids running around, not for a part-time dad who is now a bachelor. I wonder why Michael is doing all of this. Does he actually want to take care of Alice full-time? I fail to see how that would ever work with the eighty-plus hours he works per week. Does he just want her away from my influence? Am I really such a terrible mother?

Michael has systematically removed all evidence of my existence from the apartment. Every room I go through has only his belongings. Littered everywhere are objects he feels are needed to signal his success to the rest of the world. He has no photo frames with shots of the past or the family we briefly were. This place is a shrine to him and him alone.

I shake my head as I silently wish to myself that things had been different. I never wanted to break off what we had, but he could never forgive me for that day. I know he tried for a time to make things work, but our demise was inevitable. It makes me sick to my core that he couldn't work through our problems and forget what happened, for Alice's sake. I know it was asking a lot, but we could have started over.

I reach the end of the hall and step into Michael's office, with a grand view of a different angle of the city. Central Park is only a few blocks away, stretching out in either direction, lined by other tall apartment buildings, full of the elite of the city. A library of legal books dominates one wall. I wonder if Michael has read every one of them.

Alice isn't here, but there has to be something to implicate him in all of this. I approach his oversize oak desk and see little on the top except his computer, a desktop phone, and a few lamps spaced evenly apart.

The first thing I need to do, now that I know Henry has been lying to me, is call the police. I call 911 and tell them my daughter has been kidnapped by a man in the building. I leave Michael and Alan out of the picture for now, not wanting to complicate things. The operator tells me she received a call like this only a few minutes ago and that the police are on their way now. Henry has obviously decided to do the right thing.

I fall back into Michael's office chair and breathe. I lean my head back with the knowledge that soon the police will arrive and tear through the building to find Alice. When I lean forward again, I see Michael's computer is on.

I wiggle the mouse ever so gently, not wanting to move it too far from its original position. The computer is not only on, but unlocked. I can't believe my luck as I stare at a picture of Michael golfing with his lawyer buddies. I chuckle to myself as I freely access his private computer. Why would he leave it here like this? I guess he never thought someone would walk into the apartment. That, or he isn't far away. Maybe he stepped out this morning and will soon be back, as his neighbor said. I move quickly.

I need proof—something to show he planned to take Alice from me. I check his emails, making sure not to open any unread ones. I check his documents, his downloads, his search history, the files he has marked for deletion. Nothing. Not a single thing out of the ordinary.

"Bastard," I whisper. I should have known Michael wouldn't be careless enough to leave evidence lying around. His firm would have taught him better than that.

I keep searching his computer, clicking on icons at random. I know I need to move on and keep looking for Alice, but I just want a few more minutes to find something. I know Michael is behind this. He has to be.

I close everything down after another minute of fruitless searching and place the mouse where it should be. I reluctantly get up to leave Michael's study, but notice something out of the corner of my eye I swear wasn't there a moment ago. On one of the shelves off to the side of the study is a book that simply doesn't belong in the stacks of boring and thick legal bibles: *Alice's Adventures in Wonderland*. It's not Alice's copy. It's too new to be. In fact, it's still in its wrapping, as if someone had just purchased it from the shops.

I pick up the book carefully and run my fingers over the surface, feeling the connection it holds to Alice beneath the plastic layer. In my mind, I can smell the pages of Alice's copy and feel her warm body on my lap as I read to her. What I wouldn't give to be reading to her right now from the safety of our home.

What does this mean? Why does Michael have this here? Did he simply purchase something he knew would make his daughter happy, or was he planning on giving it to Alice once he had successfully taken her from me? Did he realize he would actually have to read the book when she asked him to? I think about the empty backpack downstairs and shudder at the thought.

Clearly, Michael knew that he would need a spare copy of *Alice's Adventure's in Wonderland* if he were to keep our daughter happy and content with this forced transition. It wouldn't be enough, though. She would miss me, right? A four-year-old child wouldn't just forget about the person who'd raised them their entire life, would they? I had to believe that.

I feel anger welling up inside me as I think about that creep Desmond. Why would he would risk his own skin to kidnap a little girl? How much did it take for him to cross that line? What was the going rate for a man to justify committing such a crime?

Thoughts of Michael, Desmond, and even Alan cloud my brain as I find myself wanting vengeance on all three of them.

Alan has already received some form of karma for his role in all of this. I just need the other two to suffer for what they've done.

I find myself back in the living area, where I used to spend many hours sitting on the couch while tending to Alice in her bassinet. Her first six months were the hardest time of my life, but she was worth every second.

I still remember seeing her face when they first handed her to me. How was she so soft and perfect? We come into this life so innocent and pure, only to have the world crush our spirits into dust. I shudder to think when Alice will fall victim to such cynicism.

I don't know where to go after I leave the apartment. Deep down I know that my time in here is an attempt to distract myself from facing the reality that Desmond has Alice in his possession. He has to still be somewhere in the building; somewhere that makes hiding a small child an easy task.

A memory hits me in a flash: a place I used to escape to when I lived in Michael's apartment.

"The roof," I say out loud.

She has to be there. It's close by and there is a small utility room. Enough for Michael to keep tabs on Desmond and Alice. First, I decide to call Henry and check in to see if he saw Desmond or Alice on his way down to the lobby before he called the police.

"Nothing down this way. They must still be somewhere above level seven."

"Okay, thanks," I say, before I hang up. I feel the corners of my mouth twitching into a smile. I feel more and more confident that I am honing in on Michael's plan. His efforts to take Alice away will not defeat me. Not now. Not ever.

CHAPTER 26

Then

When Alice was only six weeks old, I was informed that I was suffering from postpartum depression and anxiety. When Michael's doctor said this, the words sounded like complete nonsense, for one simple reason: they weren't true. How could I have been diagnosed with such a thing when I loved my Bunny more than anything else in the world? This man wasn't my doctor and knew none of my medical history.

From the moment I met him, I didn't trust the supposed professional my husband had paid to come visit me in the apartment. I had always seen my own doctor in Brooklyn. Now Michael was trying to make me believe I had problems, that I was some sort of unstable mother on the edge of losing it.

I refused to let him manipulate me like that and influence the way I took care of Alice. For weeks he continued this narrative, driving home his concern, until he had me starting to question my own feelings. When someone whom you once loved with all of your heart pays a doctor to tell you these things, you can't help but start to believe them.

One Sunday afternoon, when Michael got called into work, his weeks of trying to change me rolled into one big ball of pain.

Alice was crying again. It seemed that she never stopped for those first six weeks. How could such a small person make such a loud noise?

I had pulled Alice, in her bassinet, out to the living area of our oversized apartment, in an attempt to change her surroundings to see if it would help her to sleep. She was struggling to stay asleep, though that's all a newborn baby really had to get a handle on. I had read that she would sleep like a log between feeds and survive on a cycle of eating, sleeping, and pooping. She would only be awake for short times until she reached three months. That was not the case with Alice.

Michael went back to work after three weeks. He could have taken longer off, but it was evident to all concerned that he wanted to be away from the screaming baby and the frazzled wife that accompanied her. Michael made me so angry when he told me he had to return to work; we both knew he could have gotten someone in to cover for him.

"I can't lose my position at the firm," he said. "I've invested too much there to throw it all away now. I need to continue to provide for the future."

His words only served to enrage me, so I sent him back. I didn't want that around Alice. He'd been all too concerned about Alice's welfare when I was pregnant. Now that she was here, the reality of caring for a newborn hit him hard. He thought he could give his daughter what she needed by working as much as possible. It felt like a path of abandonment to me, so I did what I could to shield her from his BS in the short term.

The nurses I spoke to over the phone couldn't tell me why Alice wouldn't sleep. All I knew was how dangerous not getting enough shut-eye was for her development. As a result, I failed to take care of myself. All of my energy went into Alice, but I didn't seem to have enough.

I would go from feeling angry and full of resentment toward Michael, to a complete state of nothingness. The empty numbness was worse than the anger. At least anger was an emotion. Feeling dead inside when you thought about your husband was not how this was all supposed to go. Was his doctor right about me? Back then, I swung between being overwhelmed with pressure to feeling utterly alone. Most days I was alone.

Michael would leave early in the morning to get away from me. I was tasked with keeping our newborn alive, despite the condition he believed I had. Sure, I had tough days like any new mother did, but I wasn't depressed. I couldn't be. I did whatever was needed to care for Alice.

After what felt like one particularly long morning, Michael came home for lunch at around one, as promised. He was going to spend an hour with his family before heading back to work, away from me.

"How is everything going?" he asked as gently as he could as he approached me on the couch. Alice was crying in her bassinet.

Michael was tiptoeing around me like I was poisonous. I couldn't help my answer. It all came out in a ball of fire. "Why do you care?"

"I'm just asking. You don't have to bite my head off."

"Are you serious?" I asked. "You keep telling me that I need help, that I'm in no condition to look after my Bunny, but where are you?"

"Erika, please."

"No. Tell me. Where are you every day?" I yelled.

Michael stared at me for a long time, while my nostrils flared wide with anger.

"I have to work," he said.

"Work," I repeated. "Where you'd rather be, instead of supporting me through my supposed condition."

"Erika, please. My doctor—"

"Your doctor is full of shit. All he ever tells me is how worthless I am as a mother. Do you have any idea how insulting and painful his advice is?"

"No, but if you try listening to his advice, it will help. I promise you."

I shook my head at him. "No, Michael. Just go. Go back to your precious fucking law firm and be where you want to be." I rolled away from him on the couch, out of sight. Alice continued to wail for attention. I gently rocked the bassinet back and forward. She eased up a little, but not enough to actually stop.

"I don't *want* to be there. Not when things are this bad."

"Then why can't you take some more time off?"

"You know why. I'd lose my standing at the firm. If I lose that, we lose this apartment."

"I couldn't give a shit about this apartment. I never wanted it in the first place."

Alice's cry rang out, even louder than before. My yelling was making things worse, but Michael was provoking me.

"Thanks a lot," I said, as I bent down over the bassinet and scooped Alice up into my hands. "There, there, Bunny. It's okay." I tried to calm her crying with gentle shushing, but Alice wouldn't stop.

Michael walked over to me and held out his hands. "Can I hold her?"

I felt a slight bit of caution at his request. He was the father of our child, yet I felt anxious letting him anywhere near Alice. I shouldn't have that reaction.

I placed her in his arms and watched as he cradled her with genuine love. Love he only had for my daughter. I saw pain and anguish flow through his eyes. Did he actually care about her? He turned his body away from me too quickly.

"What are you doing?" I asked.

"I'm taking Bunny away from you."

"What do you mean? You can't take her."

He backed up a few steps, his eyes wide. He glanced around the apartment as if he was about to bolt out of the door with Alice in his hands.

"You need a few hours away from each other. I'll look after her so you can get some rest. Sound good?"

"Don't you have to work?"

"Yeah," he said, "but I'll get my assistant to look after her."

I stared at the ground for a moment and shook my head. "No. I have to be with her. I have to. All the books say so. The mother should be as close to the baby at all times during the first six months. And I don't want some stranger holding her. You can't take her from me."

I held out my hands for him to return Alice. He hesitated. I saw his gaze flick around the room. What was going on inside that head? I didn't have the time or the energy to work out what Michael was trying to achieve, so I grabbed Alice from him.

"I'm trying to help you, Erika. Clearly, you need it," he said, gesturing toward Alice.

"It's too late for you to help us," I said. "Just go back to work. We don't need you." I spun away and placed Alice back in her bassinet. She cried straight away; the sound sent a shudder down my spine.

"Forget this," he muttered.

I scoffed at Michael's ridiculous offer for someone else to take care of Alice for him. He thought he could just go out there and make a lot of money to hire people to come in and take care of Alice, but I didn't want aid from strangers. I wanted it from the loving husband that Michael should have been.

I didn't turn to face him. Instead, I hoped that he would see the damage he was doing to me with his doctors and their intentionally false diagnosis. Why was this happening?

When I heard the sound of the front door closing with a bang, I knew a significant moment in our marriage had passed. It was the beginning of the end, the mark of what was to come.

Alice cried harder than before, her wails spiraling into my brain. I got up and tried to calm her down. I lifted her out of the bassinet and tried everything, but she wouldn't stop for a single second. She could sense the anguish pulsating through my veins and reacted accordingly. I placed her gently back down and felt my temples flare with pain.

I screamed out loud as I gripped my skull and fell back to the floor, not caring where I landed. How did things get this way? How had I become the world's worst mother? A wife that drove her husband out the door? They would both be better off without me. Michael had convinced me of that.

Suddenly, Alice's cries softened and faded into the background. I swiveled around and rose from the ground. I slowly walked for the front door as Alice continued to moan behind me. She tried to scream louder, but was drowned by the deafening static that filled my head.

I continued to the front door and unlocked it. Michael thought he could just walk out of there, so I did too. After all, I wasn't a good mother, according to his doctors.

I shuffled, dead on my feet, out of the apartment, and didn't bother to lock the door. As I made my way down the corridor toward a maintenance door, I no longer heard Alice screaming. I didn't hear anything.

The next thing I knew, I was on the roof. I never thought I could get up there, but I found a way through a poorly locked door to the tall rooftop. I crept to the edge and climbed up on the brickwork. I stared down at the street below me as it begged for us to meet, to become one, to end my pain.

Was this what he wanted?

Was this what was best for us all?

I hovered one foot out, letting my center of gravity tip forward, closer to death, closer to the last moment of my life. I had always wondered about the final thought a person had before they ended it all. Did they think about their greatest regrets? Did they think about all of the things they had failed to achieve?

Only one thought came into my head at that moment: Alice. Her cries for help took over.

I pulled myself in abruptly and fell backward onto the hard rooftop as I once again heard the screams in the back of my head. "Alice," I said out loud. She needed me. I couldn't ease my pain knowing she was here in this world alone.

I rushed back down and into the apartment before anyone could see what I had just tried to do. I locked the front door and rushed to the bassinet to scoop up my Bunny. I held her close and made a promise there and then never to leave her.

CHAPTER 27

Now

I run for the front door of Michael's apartment, knowing exactly where I need to go and how to access the roof of the building. I've been there before. It seems silly that a large apartment on the Upper West Side could feel small, but it did. I had hated living here. It closed in on me quite regularly, until I had no choice but to escape its walls.

I push through an access door I know is unlocked and double back along a service tunnel to some steps I doubt the residents of Stonework Village know exists. I should have looked here sooner given who has taken Alice. I picture Desmond dragging my Bunny through here and use that image to push myself forward. The stairs take me up to the roof of the building, which is protected by a poorly locked door with a warning sign that fails to turn me around. I see that maintenance hasn't fixed the doorframe, and I push the barely secured door open with little effort.

The roof is the perfect place for a kidnapper to hide a child. I don't know why I didn't think of it earlier. I pour out onto the blazingly cold roof space and dart my head left and right to seek out Desmond.

I run around the area, bracing myself against the chill of the wind at this height. I gaze up and see several rusted water towers standing tall above, reaching into the sky. The age of the building is far more apparent up here than inside, where cosmetic work is continually being done to give the residents the impression that Stonework Village isn't as old as they think.

I rush from one side of the roof to the other. AC units and vents line the way with obstacles and trip hazards. I check the small storage room, but the only hiding place on the roof of the building is empty.

"Dammit," I yell. I twist my fingers into my hair and pull. I was positive that I would find them here. I'm fast running out of places in the building he could have taken her.

I find myself by the edge of the building with both hands planted firmly on the side of the brickwork, which reaches just above my hips. It wouldn't be hard for a person to fall off the roof. I guess people were a bit shorter when this building was first constructed.

As my hands rest on the cold surface, painful memories cloud my brain. I falter and move back a few paces as I feel my hands reach for my head again and grip tight. "No," I let out. I move away from the edge and feel the pain clear up the further back I go. Though I once came up here and considered doing something so reckless it would have changed Alice's world forever, the woman who thought about doing the unthinkable wasn't me. I could never do something so final now. Not while Alice needs me.

I push the apprehension away and stay on the task at hand. Alice isn't here, and I need to move forward to the next possible place Desmond might have taken her. But where is that?

"Excuse me," a voice calls out from behind. "What are you doing up here?"

I almost jump out of my skin when I spin around to see a maintenance man staring at me, confusion clear in his expression.

"Well? What are you doing up here? This area is off limits to the residents. Surely you saw the signs?"

I am about to ask him if he has seen my little girl, but something stops me. What if he is friends with Desmond or Alan?

"I'm sorry. I did see the signs," I confess. "I just like to come up here for the fresh air, you know?" It's the first lie I can think of.

The man in coveralls holds his ground and his gaze. His shoulders are tense and ready to do whatever is necessary to keep me out of this forbidden area. Who is he?

"I'm sorry," I repeat. "I'll go."

"No, it's fine," he says, as his shoulders drop. "You can stay. It's not like you could do much harm up here."

I let out a sigh of relief, as quietly as I can. "Thank you."

He steps toward me. "I'm Gus, by the way. Head of maintenance."

Head of maintenance? Is this the man Henry has searching the building? I realize Gus is staring at me, waiting for a response. "Erika," I say.

"Which level do you live on, Erika?"

The question makes me scream on the inside. I want to know if he's seen Alice or not, but at the same time, I don't know if I can trust him. What should I tell him? I begin to panic. "Level fourteen. Apartment 1402."

"One of the building's few top-floor owners, huh?" I can hear the disdain barely hidden in his voice. It's obvious he hates serving the elite of New York for a living. I can't say that I blame him. His efforts must go unappreciated at the best of times. The people that live at the top expect everything to always work. They throw money at their problems. It's the only way they know how to fix a complication.

I watch as Gus pulls out a pack of cigarettes. "Do you mind?" he asks, as he places a smoke in his mouth.

"No," I say, shaking my head. "Be my guest." I need to continue searching for Alice, but I also need to know if Gus has found any clues as to her whereabouts. In the same frustrating moment, I don't want this man to think I'm up to no good and follow me. I have no idea what to do.

Gus lights up and draws in a long breath of the deadly smoke. He closes his eyes when he exhales, enjoying that brief moment when his brain rewards him for giving in to his craving. It won't last long.

"Want one?" he offers.

"No, thanks. Never touch the things."

"Smart lady. In today's age, it's getting harder and harder to find a place that will let you smoke. I'm technically not allowed to do it on site—roof included. I'm supposed to go thirty feet away from the building. I don't see what the problem is if I'm up on the roof. Damn company policy."

"It's just the way things are, I guess. Maybe you should quit." I shake my head as I hear the words come out of my mouth. I sound awkward.

He stares at me through squinted eyes as he takes another drag on his cigarette. "Yeah, maybe I should. After all, a top-floor resident such as yourself would know best, right?"

I try to decipher as quickly as I can what he means by that before I respond. "No, don't listen to me. What would I know?"

"Obviously more than me, right? I mean, how else can you afford to live in a place like this?"

I feel sick saying these words, but I hope they shut him up. "My husband is quite successful. I'm a nobody. I just married the right person, I guess."

"Well, not much I can do about that, is there? My wife is a schoolteacher. She may not be rich like your husband, but I love her more than anything else in the world."

"That's nice to hear." I can see that he genuinely loves his wife. I doubt I will ever have that kind of relationship again in my life. The only person I truly care for anymore is Alice, and I need to get rid of this guy before Desmond slips away.

"Anyway," I say, "I should probably head back down."

He nods as he takes a final drag on the cigarette, as intensely as if it were his last smoke. "Gotta keep that husband of yours happy."

"Something like that," I say, as I head for the door.

"How long have you lived here?" he asks the back of my head. His question stops me short of the only exit off the roof. Luckily, he can't see my gobsmacked face as I try to think of a suitable answer.

I turn around and see Gus waiting for a response with one raised brow. "About four years."

He purses his lips and nods his head. "Four years, huh? I suppose you would have been here when we had the big fire."

I keep my reaction contained as I absorb his words, trying to determine if he is trying to catch me out in a lie. This has to be a test. I know it.

"Yes, it was a scary day, from what I remember." I point toward the door. "I'm sorry, but I really need to get going."

"Oh, don't let me hold you up," he says.

I let out a quiet breath as I head for the door again.

"Of course, I am a bit curious now, because I was under the impression that the resident in 1402 was a single man. Oh, and another thing, there's never been a big fire in the building."

I freeze on the spot, knowing I'm screwed. Gus will have no choice but to drag me out of the building.

The head of maintenance closes the gap on me. "Just who are you, really, and what are you doing up here?"

CHAPTER 28

I stare at Gus as he repeats his question. "Who are you?" His words seem to play on a loop as I stumble away, knocking into the door through which I was trying to escape.

Gus moves in closer, flicking his cigarette into the wind. He grabs me by the shoulders before I topple over. "Are you okay?"

I regain my footing and gently push his hands off of me. "I'm fine, thank you."

"What happened just now?"

"I don't know. I guess I got a bit dizzy or something."

"Okay. But dizzy or not, you still haven't answered my question. Who are you? Really? You can't be married to Michael Walls. He lives in 1402 on his own. He has for a few years now. Are you his girlfriend or something?"

I don't know what to say. Do I give him the truth? Do I tell him a bunch of lies? All I want to do is locate Desmond and save Alice from Michael and his schemes.

"Well? You've got about three seconds before I have no option but to throw you out of this building. There's a lot going on here today."

"Okay," I say, one hand on my clammy forehead. "I'll answer your questions. Just give me some space, please."

Gus complies with a frown, but stays within a close enough distance to grab me if need be. He crosses both arms over his chest, like he is a school principal waiting for an explanation from a student caught doing the wrong thing.

"I used to be married to Michael. We're divorced now. I came to the building to retrieve something for our four-year-old daughter, Alice. We were heading up to the top floor when the elevator jammed just below level seven. The doors partially opened, and my little girl got scared and ran off through the small gap."

"You're the mother whose kid has gone missing?"

"It's more complicated than that," I say.

"What do you mean?"

I let out a sigh and begin to tell him everything. I don't know what it is about Gus, but I feel compelled to confess to him what has happened today with Alice, Michael, and Alan. I explain that I am trying to find Desmond before he escapes. I also tell him about Henry and the delay he created in getting the police involved. It's a lot to understand and absorb on a good day, but Gus seems to take it all in without freaking out.

"So that's everything. Happy?"

"No," he says. "You've just made my crappy day way more complicated than it needs to be."

I slump down into myself and lower my head. I have let the burdens of my life come spewing out. I've unloaded too much at once. Gus won't believe me and will have no choice but to have me removed from the building. I can't say I blame him. I probably sound nuts.

"Are you going to kick me out?" I ask.

"Not a chance. I have a few kids of my own. I lost one of them for a few hours in Central Park one afternoon. It was the worst day of my life. I know a little bit about what you're going through, kidnapping conspiracies about your ex-husband aside. So, what are you waiting for?"

I raise my head. "What do you mean?"

"Why are you still up here when Desmond is somewhere in this building?"

"I thought that—"

"That I wouldn't believe you? I probably shouldn't, but there's always been something about Desmond that gives me the creeps. He's an extremely private person. Alan doesn't seem the sort who would get involved in something like this, but then again, I had no idea he was Desmond's father. I guess I never really knew Alan's surname to begin with, or I'd forgotten it. He was in charge here before I came along. He must have had some pull with the company to be able to hire his son like that. This explains so much."

A glimmer of hope hits me. "Really? Like what?"

"Hard to put it into words," Gus says, as he runs his fingers over his thin mustache. "Desmond doesn't really talk to you when you say hello or ask how his day is going. He never comes out of his apartment that often, except to work. He looks broken on the inside or something. I often suspected he might have done some time."

"So you worked it out. How long have you thought that he might be an ex-con?"

"A few months. Desmond has only been on the job for half a year. He struck me as odd on day one."

"Okay," I say, as I nod my head and pace around. "So where would he hide a little girl in this building?"

Gus frowns in thought. "I've already searched the corridors of every floor, as Henry requested, but there are some empty apartments on seven."

"I think he was headed there, but I scared him back up the building. What else?"

"If he's not in an apartment, there's some crawl space behind the elevator shaft on every level. If he managed to go back down, there's also the garage. It's small, but it has a storage room."

I breathe out loud with a huff. "That's a lot of places. I'll try the elevator crawl space first." I turn around and place one hand on the door handle.

"Wait, you can't just run off like that. This guy is dangerous. He's an ex-con who may have agreed to kidnap a little girl."

"I know he's dangerous. Like I said, I've already chased him once today. I am prepared to throw myself in harm's way to get my little girl back in one piece. You can't stop me from going after him."

"Okay, okay," he says, palms raised. "But I'm coming with you. You don't even know how to access the crawl space. Plus, if Desmond were to harm anyone on my watch, there's no way I could live with myself."

I turn back to Gus and stare into his eyes for a moment. "Thank you. This means a lot to me. You have no idea what I've been through today."

"Hey, I get it. I know I'd do anything to help one of my kids. Come on," Gus says, as he moves past me and opens the flimsy door that leads back inside. "We've got an asshole to catch."

I take one last look around the roof and feel a shudder run down my spine before I go back through the door. I should feel happy that I now have the help of someone with maintenance knowledge of the building, but the memories of the roof have me on edge.

The feeling doesn't go until the door closes behind me.

CHAPTER 29

Gus leads the way from the roof of the building and down through to a narrow service tunnel that leads to the elevators, and I follow a few paces behind, silently praying that he can help me find Desmond in this awful place. His desire to get involved in my problem seems legitimate enough, and hopefully having a man from maintenance on my side will help me track down where Desmond is keeping Alice.

My mind flicks to Michael and where he is hiding today. I'd imagine he scheduled a client at the office to give himself the perfect alibi for the day. He is just waiting for me to fail to find Alice so he can show up and produce her to the authorities like some sort of heroic father. I won't let that happen.

I wonder if Desmond realizes that Michael will burn him the first chance he gets. I can picture it all now. Michael pretends to hear about the kidnapping for the first time. He searches the building frantically and finds Desmond. He produces his co-conspirator to the police, explaining how he found the ex-con holding his daughter hostage. The cops arrest Desmond while Michael emerges victorious. I feel sick thinking about it.

Gus clears his throat. "I've been in this job for three years now and in the industry for about ten. Never had to help anyone find their kidnapped girl before."

"I'm sorry," I say to Gus. I don't know what else to tell him.

"Don't be. This isn't your doing. It's the work of the devil, if you ask me. I don't know how else people can do things like this." He turns back to me in the narrow space. "Do you believe in God, Erika?"

I notice Gus is rubbing a crucifix that has come out from his coveralls. "I used to, once upon a time, but life showed me that God couldn't be real. Why else would things fall apart the way they do?"

He purses his lips. "I get where you're coming from. God tested me that day in the park. But when I found my little one safe and sound, I knew it was because of Him."

I nod and don't give Gus another word. I turn my head and let out a sigh of frustration. I went to church as a child and believed in God for the longest time. My loss of faith came about after the demise of my marriage with Michael. After that, no one can ever convince me that our lives mean anything to a holy deity in the sky. Now, I only have faith in my daughter and the love I hold for her.

We come through a section of the service tunnel I didn't know existed and out behind the elevator shaft. There is a metal walkway, which must allow maintenance workers to access the elevator from each floor. We are currently on level fourteen, and we'll need to check every floor, one by one, to do this right.

I peek down through the grate to see if I can spot Desmond or Alice, but it's too hard to spy beyond the next level below.

"I can climb down from here using a ladder that goes between floors, if you'd like, and check out every section," Gus says.

I snap my eyes to him. "Won't he hear you coming, though? We've made enough noise as it is."

Gus scratches at his chin. "That's a good point. My best bet will be to go down each floor of the building and approach the sections from the side."

Before I agree and encourage the man to help me, I realize how dangerous this idea could be for him. I have to say something. "Gus, wait. Desmond might be armed. He's an ex-con, as you know, and might know how to get a weapon off the street."

Gus rubs at his chin. "You're right. I guess we really need the police here."

"They're on their way. Hopefully they'll get here soon."

I turn away from Gus. We've hit another dead end. There's still the garage storage to be searched, along with any empty apartments, but I realize those areas also have the same problem: Desmond. If he is waiting for us with a weapon in hand, he'll attack the first one through the door. That's when my last desperate idea floods my brain. It's a stupid one, but it's all I have.

"I'm going down," I say to Gus.

"I thought you said it was too noisy? And dangerous."

"It is dangerous—for you. Not for me. Desmond can assault me however he sees fit. It won't stop me from trying to find Alice. If you follow behind at a safe distance, you can see where he is if he attacks me."

"You can't be serious?" Gus asks.

I nod without breaking my gaze. "You said yourself that you'd do anything for your kids. I'm no different."

Gus shakes his head. "I don't like it, but I understand. And I won't let you do this alone."

I'm amazed that he would do this for me. Is it even possible for someone to be this nice? Does his faith compel him to risk his own life in order to help others? All the faith in the world won't save Alice if Desmond takes me out, but I have no other choice.

"We can't both go in headfirst," I say. "You need to be able to report Desmond to the police and get help to Alice if things go wrong. We can't both draw him out from the shadows."

Gus nods and runs his fingers through what's left of his hair. "Okay. You are one brave lady."

"I'm not," I say. "I'm just a mom who's had to fight the world on her own to survive."

CHAPTER 30

Then

Alice had just hit the three-month mark. It was a significant milestone for a newborn to survive those first dangerous months of existence. Never was there a higher chance of her falling asleep and never waking up again. The thought kept me awake most of the time.

Her sleeping problem sorted itself out once I got my act together and ignored everything Michael's doctor said to me. I started my Bunny on a better routine and she fell into line almost instantly. By two months, she was sleeping the way she was meant to, for around sixteen hours per day with little effort. It was like someone had flicked a switch in Alice's brain, and now she understood what she needed to do when I put her down in her bassinet, all wrapped up. I couldn't have been more relieved to be able to get in some rest of my own whenever Alice went down for a nap.

Michael was still busy working most days. He'd only show his face to spend time with his daughter or to say goodbye to her before he left for work. He'd stand over the bassinet and place his hand down beside Alice. He'd stare at her with a look in his eyes that made me feel invisible. Throughout the day, he'd text me to check up on things. He didn't work the depression angle anymore. Instead, he made it clear that he didn't trust I could care for our daughter.

Later, he'd come home at some awful hour and say goodnight to Alice in the same loving manner. Then he'd move around the apartment as if I didn't exist.

Our relationship was never going to recover from the damage it had sustained. There were too many unrepairable hairline cracks through its core—some visible, some buried beneath the layers. At that point, we were not husband and wife. We were not a mother and a father. We were two people who shared an apartment and cared for a newborn.

I had managed to move Alice's bassinet back to the main bedroom. I liked to keep her nearby when I slept so I could be there the second she woke up. Michael slept in one of the other bedrooms and would only come into mine to get a look at Alice. He was checking up on my ability to look after our child. I shouldn't have been surprised by his lack of faith. He had micromanaged the pregnancy to the point I felt more stressed out by him than anything else. The worst part was that he was oblivious to the effect his behavior had on me. Then, on top of everything else, he tried to blame me for what happened at her birth. Up until then, he hadn't said a word about it. He had just judged me with his cold eyes.

Our new sleeping arrangements drastically reduced the amount of time I saw him, to the point where it felt like days went by between words. I virtually had no husband. How long could things continue on that path?

It was late morning, and Alice had just finished her feed and was about to go down for a nap after burping. In the bedroom, I prepared her for sleep in a stretchy green wrap that would hold her arms in place so I could put her down on her back. She was yet to try and roll over, and seemed happy to have her arms crossed over her body while she slept.

I decided to quickly duck out to the kitchen to grab a bite to eat to keep my energy levels up. I heard Michael out in the

living area, saying my name to another person. I spotted him a
moment later in the lounge with a guest. They both turned to
me the second I came into view. I froze on the spot.

"Hello," Michael said to me, his voice low and uninviting.

"Hi," I replied. That was the extent of most of our interac-
tions—on a good day. "Don't mind me," I said, as I continued to
walk toward the kitchen, allowing the two busy men to continue
their discussion. Why my name had come up at all was none
of my concern. I figured the man was a client and Michael was
trying to pretend he had a happy family at home.

"Actually, Erika, I was hoping you had a moment to meet my
friend here," Michael said.

What now? I stopped halfway to the kitchen and turned to
face our guest. He was a balding man in his late forties with a
pair of round glasses perched low upon his nose. The man stood
and walked toward me with an extended hand.

I took a few cautious steps toward him and held out my hand.
He gripped it gently and introduced himself.

"Donnie Preston," he said.

"Erika Walls," I replied.

A moment of awkward silence filled the gap between us. I had
no idea who he was or why Michael wanted me to meet him.

"And how is Bunny doing?" he asked.

I paused for a brief second. I didn't like the fact that Michael
had shared Alice's nickname with this stranger. I don't know why,
but that hurt me more than Michael ignoring me for days on end.
"She's just gone down for her nap. Are you one of Michael's clients?"

Michael scoffed in the background, apparently unimpressed
with my attitude. I didn't care, though. I didn't have the motiva-
tion or patience to meet one of the criminal clients that Michael
was paid a ridiculous sum of money to represent. This guy didn't
look the sort to have committed anything too serious, but looks
could be deceiving.

"I'm not one of his clients. I'm a friend."

He looked too old to be a friend. All I could imagine was that this man had some important connection Michael wanted to exploit.

"Well then, pleased to meet you, Donnie," I said. "If you don't mind, I've got some food waiting to be eaten in the kitchen. I only have about an hour and a half before Bunny is up again." I walked away from Donnie, not caring if I was a rude host or not. I didn't invite him here. He was not my guest to entertain.

"Erika," Michael snapped.

I directed my eyes at him with a scowl. I didn't appreciate being spoken to in such a way. "What?"

He took a moment to catch his breath and compose himself. "Why don't you sit down and join us?"

"I really just want to eat. I don't mean to be rude, but—"

"Erika, please. Just for a minute."

I huffed and pouted like a child, stomped toward the lounge, and threw myself down in one of the free armchairs. I didn't want to sit near Michael. Even the sight of him made me angry. It wasn't how a wife should feel about her husband, but I was confident Michael felt the same about me.

"I'm here. What is it you want to discuss?"

Donnie took the lead. "I haven't exactly been honest with you, Erika. When I told you my name, I neglected to tell you that I am a doctor."

"What? Like from a hospital?" I didn't want to hear more of Michael's BS about depression.

"Not exactly. I specialize in counseling and couples' therapy."

My eyes almost popped out of my head. Had Michael just sprung a therapy session on me? It was no secret we were having problems, but why didn't he discuss the idea with me first?

"Couples' therapy?" I asked. It was too little, too late, as far as I was concerned.

"I'm sorry," Michael said, "but it was going to be too hard to go anywhere with, you know—"

"With our baby?"

Michael held his head in his hands. "You don't have to say it like that, but yes, we can't go anywhere at the moment."

"Well, I'm so sorry we are such an inconvenience to you, Michael."

Michael went to reply, but the doctor chimed in. "Erika, please. Michael has come to me with concerns about you and your relationship with him. If you could try and keep an open mind throughout and let him say his piece, we'll get through this a lot more smoothly."

I shook my head and stayed quiet. I wanted to yell at them both, but I didn't want to wake Alice. I slumped down and crossed my arms tightly over my chest. This was not how I had planned to utilize Bunny's naptime.

"Shall we begin?" Donnie asked. He glanced at Michael and then me and back again. Michael said yes. I gave them both a shrug. It was the best they were going to get.

"Okay. As far as I can see, the two of you are not talking to one another unless absolutely necessary. Why is that? What has caused this? Before either of you answer, I'm going to allow you each to respond with your own thoughts. I want to make it clear that no one interrupts the other. Go it?"

"Fine by me," I said.

"Got it," Michael said.

Donnie nodded to both of us. "Very well. Michael, why don't you answer first."

"Alright," Michael said. He leaned forward and held both hands together. I could see his mind ticking over to try and think of the right words. For a lawyer, he seemed to be having trouble coming up with the right thing to say. Had our relationship stumped him that much?

"If I'm honest, our breakdown in communication started the day Erika went into labor."

My eyes almost bulged out of my head. We'd had problems before then. And how could he refer to that moment to highlight something negative? I went to jump in, but Donnie anticipated this and held up a hand to remind me to bite my tongue. It pained me to do so, but I let Michael continue.

"And what was it about that day that made things so difficult between you both?"

Michael's mouth twisted into an ironic smile, but his eyes were welling up. He shook his head. "Ever since that day, Erika has only focused on Bunny, and not the problems anyone can clearly see she is having. I know things changed a lot in that moment, but I…" He trailed off and lowered his head until no one could see his face.

"That's okay, Michael. Take a minute to think." Donnie turned to me. "And you, Erika, what was it about that day that caused you to have tension with Michael?"

I uncrossed my arms and leaned closer to the doctor. "It was more than a bit of tension; I was frightened of him."

"Frightened?"

"Yes. After her birth, I knew he'd be upset and disappointed with how our Bunny came into the world. I knew everything would be my fault, and that I'd get the blame for the emergency birth and for not doing the right things during my pregnancy. Well, I know what you want to hear, so I'll just come out and say it: it was my fault; I screwed up. Is that better? God, I never wanted things to go that way either, but they did." I could feel my heart racing in my chest. My voice was too loud and I realized too late that my hands were flailing about.

Alice gave out a long wail, having been abruptly woken more than an hour before she naturally would. I cursed under my breath. "Great. Now I've woken her up."

Michael and Donnie glanced at each other as I jumped to my feet and headed for the bedroom.

"Erika?" Donnie said.

I paused, but my impatience was clear. This doctor had less than ten seconds to get out whatever it was that he wanted to say.

"Why don't you leave her for a moment, huh? I'm sure she'll be okay."

"Are you serious? She's crying because I woke her with my loud words; words that you encouraged to come out of me."

Michael tried to cut in. "Erika, please—"

"No. Don't try and quiet me down to make yourself look better. I'm trying to express myself here. Isn't that what all of this crap is supposed to be about?"

Alice cried harder, begging for my attention. I went to leave again.

"Erika," Donnie said. "Please come back and sit down for thirty seconds. If she doesn't settle in that time, you can leave."

I threw up my hands. "Fine, but this is a waste of time." I walked away from the crying, back to the lounge. I sat down on the edge of my seat, ready to get up and go.

"Close your eyes and focus on your breathing."

I looked at Donnie like he was the most prominent moron in the world. "Okay, but this won't help." I closed my eyes and focused on my lungs, filling them with air and emptying them after a held count, the way I had learned in the yoga classes I never attended anymore. As if by magic, Alice settled. I turned to Donnie. "You got lucky."

"It was worth a shot," he said. "Now, you have both answered my first question honestly, in the way you each interpret things to be. I want to ask you another question, and again, I want Michael to answer first."

"Fine," I said.

"Go ahead," Michael replied.

"Very well. What are you each afraid is going to happen?"

Michael leaned back into his seat and put his hands on his head as he let out a long sigh. "A lot of things. I'm scared that I'll lose my job, that we'll lose this apartment. But most of all, if I'm absolutely honest, I'm scared we'll lose everything we've built together, that all of these years we've been a couple has been for nothing."

Donnie nodded while I did what I could to contain the many questions I wanted to throw at Michael. Was he acting in front of Donnie to show he cared about our marriage? We both knew he didn't. I had to do everything within my power to keep my cool.

"And you, Erika? What are you afraid is going to happen?"

I stared at the doctor as my mind span around in circles. I thought about giving some generic answer just to satisfy whatever it was that this session was supposed to achieve, but instead, the truth came into my thoughts and wanted to spill out into the world.

I thought about the last three months, and Michael's approach to Alice and me. The way he stared at her and leaned over the bassinet, ignoring me like I was worthless, told me my answer.

I stared at Donnie. "I'm scared Michael is going to take my Bunny away from me."

CHAPTER 31

Now

An echo bounces off the wall of the elevator crawl space. Gus shows me the ladder between levels and how to open each access point to head down to the next section. It's a crazy plan, but it's the best way for us to rule out the elevator shaft as a hiding spot.

I try to move without making a lot of noise, but it's near impossible. The movements of the elevator, as well as a loud, continuous hum, drown out some of the sounds, but the metal hinges are too rusty and old to be completely silent.

The elevator is sitting on floor thirteen, waiting for its next command. The back of the elevator looks unsafe; I feel nervous just being near it. I keep my fears from Gus, not wanting to worry him.

I climb down the fixed metal ladder to level thirteen. I had already scouted ahead and couldn't see Desmond there. I squint through the grate below my feet, but I won't be able to see the next level down until I reach the floor.

My feet land on the catwalk louder than I wanted them to. The noise will travel and potentially spook Desmond if he is on any of the floors below. "Come on. You can do this," I tell myself in a whisper. I think about Alice. If she's down here, she is being forced to hide behind the very thing that caused her to run in the first place. Her small belly will be churning away with the sight of the elevator going up and down.

I refocus and drop to the grated floor as quickly as I can to spy down to the next section. Twelve looks clear, so I open the ladder hatch and cringe as it creaks and squeals out for lubricant. Gus is not far behind, staying one level above me at all times. If I get attacked by Desmond, so be it. At least Gus will know precisely where the ex-con is hiding Alice, and he'll be able to do something about it.

I am prepared to die for Bunny. I know most parents say they'd do anything for their children, but would they make the ultimate sacrifice when push came to shove? Would they give up everything just to give their child a fighting chance? I know I would. Would Michael? He would probably just pay someone to do the dying for him. It's how he solves all of his problems.

I reach twelve and find an identical setup. I repeat the process and drop down to spy ahead. Nothing suspicious meets my eyes.

We keep up this rhythm until I reach level nine. I look down through the grate below. I see a blurry figure beyond the next few levels of catwalk, standing on the seventh floor. At least I think I see something. Whatever it is, it's moving.

I look up to Gus and hold a finger to my lips to make sure he stays silent. I point out there is a person below. He moves down to my level and takes a look. He spots them moving around in the same section as well. Neither of us says a word as we try to decipher what it is we are witnessing.

It has to be Desmond. Unless it's another maintenance worker I haven't met, there's no one else who would have a reason to be back here like we are. I try to confirm my suspicions with a few whispered words.

"How many maintenance people are working today?"

"You're looking at him. Most days there's three of us on the schedule, but my co-workers called in sick. No one offered to cover."

I scoff at my luck. Of all the days for two people to call in sick… I need all the help I can get to go against Michael.

I glance down again two levels below before looking over to Gus. "So who is that, then? No one should be back here except us or Desmond."

Gus takes a good hard look down with squinted eyes. "They aren't in uniform. I can't make out if it's Desmond or not. We need to move down to the next level."

"Okay," I say, barely audible enough to hear the word myself. I remember that Desmond was wearing casual clothing when he ran away from Henry and me.

I creep to the ladder and open the hatch for access. The figure below starts to pace back and forth as I lower myself down. This has to be Desmond. I can feel it in my bones.

I reach eight and quietly drop down to my hands and knees to spy through the grate. Sure enough, I see Desmond moving back and forth along the catwalk. "Got you," I whisper to myself. My next concern is to spot Alice. I look around, trying to spy past the metal grate as best I can, until I find a pair of small shoes off to the side of the catwalk. "Alice," I say, welling up. She's right there, so close I feel like I could reach out and touch her.

She's sitting on a box. I can only see her legs from the knees down. Her coat almost reaches that length when she is standing, as I decided to buy one that would last a few years. I could have used Michael's child support to buy her a new coat every year, but any extra money I didn't spend went straight into a bank account for Alice, so she could one day afford to go to college.

Gus catches up with me and spots Desmond the second he spies through the grate. He shakes his head at him in disgust. I point out Alice's legs. The second Gus sees them, his hand flies up to cover his mouth. The confirmation that Desmond has taken a little girl is almost too much for him to handle. "Son of a bitch," he mutters.

"What do we do?" I ask. "I don't see a weapon. How can we get down there without tipping him off?" I'm amazed he hasn't heard us yet. Fortunately, I doubt Desmond is expecting anyone to approach him from above or below like this. He must be too focused on the plan, whatever that is.

"You take the stairs down to the next level and make your way in from the side to grab Alice and run," Gus says. "As soon as I see you, I'll make a distraction from above."

I nod with a grimace. It's the best plan I've heard all day. Desmond won't see it coming, either. As far as he knows, the police are on their way to search the building for a missing child. He doesn't realize they are now coming to arrest a kidnapper. Whatever made him use the elevator earlier with Alice must have been important. I can't imagine him leaving the area anytime soon. We can take our time and do this right. If we time it correctly, we'll scare him away from Alice, right into the approaching police officers.

"Ready when you are," I say to Gus.

"Alright. You make your way across and down while I stay up here. I'll keep my eyes on Alice. As soon as I see you take her, I'll make as much noise as I possibly can. Desmond will be so spooked, he won't know where to look."

"Easy," I say. I walk silently along the catwalk and keep my eyes trained on Alice. Or on her legs, at least. Gus stays where he is to provide a distraction from above Desmond. I spot the oversize wrench hanging off the end of a toolbox in my path a second too late. I step right into it, bashing the tool on my shin. The wrench falls off the box and makes an almighty crashing sound when it hits the metal grate as I drop down in a failed attempt to catch it.

I snap my head below to see Desmond staring up at us with surprise in his eyes. He runs before I can say a word, grabbing Alice by the hand. I hear him command her to run with him, back through the side of the service area and out of sight.

"No!" I yell, as I scramble to my feet and chase after them. I pull the ladder hatch up with a yank and force my feet down onto the first rung. I half fall down the hole and land awkwardly with a thud.

"What are you doing?" Gus yells down to me, as I take off after Desmond.

CHAPTER 32

There's no way I'm letting Desmond out of my sight as I bash and squeeze my way through the service tunnel on level seven. He is only a short distance away, pulling Alice by the hand. I can picture her little legs trying hard to keep up while he yanks her along by the arm. Every ounce of pain he inflicts on my daughter will come back to him in double, I swear it. I will replace my fear with rage.

Gus is too far behind to be of use, so I ignore his yelling. I didn't see a gun in Desmond's possession, so I don't slow down. He could shoot at me all he wanted, though, and I'd still give chase until I drew my last breath. No one can stop me from saving my Bunny from Michael's plans. I will get her back from this awful building, no matter the cost.

I spill out the service door, which is beside the elevator, and look left and right. I can't see Desmond or Alice. At this point, he could be heading to his apartment, Alan's apartment, or one of the empty ones. My best option is to make as much noise as I can and try to force Desmond out from hiding. This has gone on long enough.

I bash on the first door I see and shout his name. "Desmond! Open up." I move along, knocking three times with a balled-up fist on each door as I continue to shout. "Desmond, come out! I know you're here. You can't hide from me any longer."

After pounding on a few doors, one behind me opens up. The older lady I spotted gawking at me earlier before pokes her head out with a scowl to see what all the fuss is about.

"You again," she says. "Why are you making all this racket?"

"I need to find Desmond. Did you see him come by here at all? He's taken my daughter."

She looks shocked at this piece of information. "Desmond?"

"Yes. He took my little girl. I need to find him, right now."

The woman looks me up and down with a squint. "Come on in, dear. I think I can help you."

"Thank you," I say, letting out a sigh of relief. I follow into her apartment, which smells of vegetable soup. She takes entirely too long to move through the small entryway just outside the kitchen area. I don't bother to close her front door—I'll be out of here and continuing my search any minute.

"Did you see them come by?" I ask.

"We'll get to that, dear. Just follow me."

I comply, but I'm dancing on the spot like I'm desperate to use the restroom. I take a look back at the front door and consider running back out and leaving the old woman behind. I don't have time for this.

"If you haven't seen them, that's fine. I really need to—"

"One moment, dear," she says, as she rummages through a drawer in the kitchen. I don't know what the hell this is all about. I need to go. This was a terrible idea, I suddenly realize. Time is evaporating before my eyes.

"I'm going to go," I say.

The woman shuffles back to me and reaches out. She grabs my right hand with both of her own. "Nonsense, dear. You need to take a moment to slow down."

I stare into her eyes as she cups my hand between hers. What is this? I get my answer a moment later when I hear the click of the handcuff around my wrist. Before I can react, she connects the other end to a pipe that is fixed to the radiator panel close to the kitchen.

"What are you doing?" I yell, while the old lady backs away with crossed arms and a smug expression.

I yank hard on the cuffs and instantly feel their strength. "You don't understand. I need to find Desmond before it's too late."

"You'll do no such thing. I'm calling the police."

"What? No, you need to listen to me. Desmond has—"

"Keep your mouth shut," she says to me with a raised voice, pulling out a cell phone that has to be around five years old. "I'm calling the police so they can take you away."

"You don't understand what you're doing. Desmond has—"

"Desmond is probably just trying to get away from you and your lies," she says. "You must be harassing him. He would never take someone's little girl, so I'm going to have you arrested so you leave that nice young man alone."

I pull harder and harder on the cuffs, hurting myself in the process. Why does this old bat have handcuffs in her kitchen drawer? I don't have time to work out why. I realize Gus will have no idea where I am unless he walks right by her door. I have no choice but to get through to this woman before she hits me over the head with a rolling pin.

"Desmond has taken my daughter. He has her with him right now. I was trying to find him before he—"

"I don't want to hear it," the woman says, as she waits on the line for the emergency services.

"Are you serious?" I ask. Either this woman is an idiot, or she has a thing for Desmond. It doesn't matter which explanation is closest to the truth; she thinks I'm the enemy and won't be happy until the police arrive.

The police will be here any moment now to speak to Henry as it is. He will fill them in and make sure that they know I'm not the bad guy here. The only problem is that he doesn't know where I am. I should have borrowed that cell phone again. Stupid. All the while, Alice is still with Desmond, their whereabouts now unknown.

I have no chance of getting out of these cuffs with the old woman staring at me. She obviously thinks I'm some deranged troublemaker, coming into her world to make things difficult for poor Desmond. If only she knew the truth.

"Hello, Mrs. Stellar here. I would like the police to come to my apartment, please," the old lady says. She continues to give them her details and goes on to explain that I am trespassing on private property—despite the fact that she invited me into her apartment. She tells the operator how she has bravely handcuffed me to her radiator. I hear her responding to some piece of information from the police. I hope they're explaining that they're already on their way to the building in regard to a kidnapping.

"That's a false call," she says. "The woman who made that claim is not to be trusted."

My heart skips a beat, and I pray the police don't take this crazed woman seriously. Somehow, the old lady can't seem to make the connection that Desmond is the reason behind the need for the authorities to be rushed out, no matter what I say.

I shake my head and tug on the cuffs again and again. I need to get out of these things if I am to have even half a chance of finding Alice.

CHAPTER 33

I gaze down at the handcuffs secured to my wrist and rattle them against the metal of the radiator pipe while Mrs. Stellar continues to stare at me. She has finished speaking to the police, who were already inbound. I can imagine the officers trying to work out what the hell is going on at Stonework Village. First, there is a kidnapping; now there is an old lady telling them that isn't true, but that there is a dangerous individual restrained in her apartment.

"You don't have to do this," I say, as I lean toward her. "I'm not a threat to you. I'm just trying to find Desmond and get my daughter back."

The old lady crosses her arms tighter. "I know that nice young man well, dear. He wouldn't do anything like that. There's no lying your way out of this one with stories about kidnapping." She places the key to the cuffs down on the counter beside her.

I shake my head and try to contain my incredulity. "You have no idea what you are talking about. Desmond is the one who should be in handcuffs. As I said, he's taken my daughter."

The old lady dismisses me with a flailing of her arms. "Lies. It's women like you who make men afraid to leave their own homes these days. I rarely get to see that nice young man. He's probably scared of people like you, throwing around accusations and causing trouble."

I realize there is no getting through to this demented crone. She has come to her own conclusions and won't see me in any other light. Desmond, for whatever reason, is her hero. I am her villain.

I have nothing else I can use to get through to her. My only option is to break this radiator pipe and run away before the police arrive.

I test the strength of the pipe by pulling hard in different locations and directions. I can see a few spots that are weaker than the rest and decide to focus on them.

"You won't break that off, dear. That pipe has only just been replaced. Desmond did it himself. If you are innocent as you claim to be, then you'll do your best to stay put and not make this any worse for yourself."

I sigh heavily and stop trying to break the pipe free from the wall. "I'm not your enemy," I say. "I'm a mother, just like you." I point my free hand to a framed photograph of two boys that sits on the kitchen counter. The old lady flicks her eyes to the photo and picks it up carefully.

"My two boys. They were such nice young men. Always coming to see their dear old mom."

I hear the woman using past tense and realize the two are either deceased or out of her life. I have no way of knowing what the answer is unless she says more. Instead of revealing more information to me, she just stares longingly at the picture and smiles.

I have to keep the conversation going. "You don't see them anymore? That must be hard for you."

Her eyes snap to mine. A slight wave of confusion fills her brow, as if she has forgotten she has a woman handcuffed to a pipe in her kitchen. "It is hard, but it's not their fault. They shouldn't have been driving that day. I should have told them to take the subway instead. It's my fault they aren't here." I see the pain in her eyes and understand that her sons died in some sort of car accident. I don't probe as to where her husband is.

"They look like they were good boys," I say, trying to appeal to her one giant weakness. I can see why she has taken a liking to Desmond. He's a dead ringer for one of the boys in the photo, though he is at least ten years older.

"They were lovely young men. Both had wonderful futures ahead of them, once they finished college. They were going to achieve astonishing things. I just knew it in my heart."

I let a moment of silence pass by before I speak. "I'm sorry for your loss."

Mrs. Stellar smiles at me as she holds the frame closer to her body. I feel like I could ask her to let me go and she wouldn't give it another thought. That possibility disappears the second she spots the handcuffs again.

"Don't try and play me, dear. My two boys were probably distracted by deceitful harlots like yourself." She places the frame carefully down. "Don't think you can trick your way out of here." The old lady looks to the open door of her apartment. "Any minute now, the police will be here to take you away."

I wonder how accurate that is, given how long the police have taken to respond. Had enough time passed for the authorities to arrive? I want the police here, but not to arrest me. Desmond will be long gone to his next hiding place by now. I'll never find him. I push the image of Alice, scared out of her wits, from my head for a moment, so I can concentrate and be free of this mess.

"You made me leave the door open," Mrs. Stellar says, as she shuffles her way to the front door. I try to think on my feet as I realize the open door is the only way for Gus or anyone else to see me in here before the police arrive. If another resident were to see me like this, would they take my side or Mrs. Stellar's? Either way, it's better for me if that door remains open.

"What were your sons studying at college?" I ask out of desperation.

The old woman spins around, fond memories filling her mind as she gives up on her idea to close the door for the time being. She is still close to the front of the apartment.

"Well, Jude was always keen to become an engineer, while Joseph was focusing on business."

"That's interesting. And were they attending the same school?"

"Yes. They were only a little over a year apart and almost inseparable. I couldn't believe it when they both managed to get into the same school one year after each other. It was amazing news to tell the rest of the family."

I can picture her gloating at the end of the year in her Christmas letter to the rest of her family. She seems the type to boast incessantly about her sons' achievements.

"They were top of their classes, you know. Always striving for the best. Never settling for second place."

I doubt this is true. Judging by the photo, her sons passed away a long time ago, maybe ten years or more. Her memory of the time could have been warped to cast her sons as a pair of perfect angels who could do no wrong. But at some point, they had been involved in a car crash. Were they to blame? Had they been drinking that night? I could only guess. But if so, that fact would have been erased from her brain along with every other fault they had exhibited.

The old lady lets out a long breath as she stares at the ceiling and turns around. She hustles over to the front door and reaches out to close it just as Gus steps into the frame.

"Mrs. Stellar," Gus says, "have you seen—"

His words stop the second he sees me waving with my cuffed hand. "What's going on here?" he asks Mrs. Stellar.

"This harlot is trying to harass poor Desmond, so I called the police to come take her away."

Gus pieces together the scene before him and asks politely to come in. Mrs. Stellar lets him in without question, possibly delighted by the company. It's quite likely the most interaction she's had with anyone in a long time.

I wonder if I'll be like her when I'm old. Will I be on my own once Alice leaves the house, slowly waiting for death to release me from my crippling loneliness?

"Would you like something to drink?" she asks Gus.

"No, thank you. What I would like is to take this woman off your hands and have her wait for the police downstairs."

"Oh no, I'm happy to help. Besides, she's not going anywhere with those on."

"I can see that. Still, I don't want you in any danger."

I try not to feel insulted as they discuss what to do with me, like I'm a rabid dog. I can see what Gus is trying to do, but Mrs. Stellar appears to be one determined old bat.

Gus stares at me and shrugs as the old lady shuffles around the kitchen. I direct his eyes to the handcuff keys on the counter. He sees them and gives me a wink.

"Are you sure you don't want anything, Gus?"

"You know what, I will have a drink. I'd love a coffee, thanks."

The task lights up Mrs. Stellar's eyes. She probably loved serving her family when her two sons were younger. The simple pleasure of preparing a coffee for her guest will keep her mind distant and distracted while Gus steals the keys.

He swivels around and places his body in front of the keys. He slowly steps back and secures them in one hand. Mrs. Stellar turns around as he approaches me. "Sugar? Milk?"

"Yes, to both. Two sugars, thanks."

She spins away and busies herself with the coffee. I doubt that's how Gus takes his coffee, but the order is enough of a distraction to allow him to pass me the key. I don't waste a second and undo the cuff. I rub my wrist while Gus steps forward and blocks Mrs. Stellar's view of me.

She moves toward him and hands over a piping hot cup of coffee. He takes a decent gulp of the steaming liquid and lets out a breath of gratitude. "Thank you. That's lovely."

I take the only opportunity I will have to leave and run for the door, key in hand.

"Oh no!" Gus says as I run away. "Don't worry, I'll go after her," he yells, as I rush off down the corridor.

I don't stop until I am around the next corner. "Don't let her get away," Mrs. Stellar shouts. I wait for Gus to catch up to me. We hurry further down the hallway until I can hide behind a support column.

"What is her problem?" I ask the second we can speak.

"Sorry about that," Gus says, as I catch my breath. "She's not all there, as you can tell."

I shake my head and focus on my breathing. "Now what?"

"Now we find Desmond."

CHAPTER 34

Then

I started packing our bags the second Michael left for work. I knew I should have waited at least an hour, but I couldn't help myself. We had to go.

"Everything is going to be okay, Bunny," I said to Alice, as she stared back at me from her bouncer. She cooed and made bubbles with her mouth, utterly oblivious to the massive change I was about to throw into her six-month-old life. She didn't deserve to have so much drama around her, but what could I do? We had to go. I no longer felt happy in this marriage, and the negativity was spilling over and into Alice's developing brain.

It wasn't just my lack of happiness driving me out the door. It pained me to think it, but I knew Michael was preparing to do something drastic himself. I could sense it in the way he spoke to me and the way he ignored my every action in the apartment. He would ask me constantly how Bunny was doing, but never how I was coping. Our marriage was on the brink of collapse, and he could only ever check up on his child.

The impromptu counseling session wasn't an isolated incident. Every week, that man returned and tried to dismantle every decision I made regarding Alice's welfare. It took me some time to realize it, but Michael was using the doctor to build a case against me. He wanted Alice taken out of my care.

He knew I didn't trust him anymore. How could I? Several times now he had offered to take Bunny off my hands to give me some time off to myself. Every time he said it, he told me he would take Alice out for the afternoon, away from the apartment and away from me. He never offered to stay in with her while I went out instead. I was convinced he had plans to take Alice from me and run away. Where he would go, I had no idea. My best guess was to his parents on Long Island, to leave Alice in their custody. They visited on occasion and also only ever seemed to be concerned for Alice and no one else. They tiptoed around me the way Michael did.

It didn't take a genius to work out that we were having issues. Anyone could see it if they merely looked for more than five seconds. Michael's parents just tried to sweep the whole thing under the rug, as if it was normal for a married couple to have a complete breakdown in communication once a child came into the picture. Maybe that was their experience, but it wasn't something I planned on putting up with for long.

I finished packing both my overnight bag and Alice's diaper bag with as many items as I could carry. I unclipped Bunny from the bouncer and lifted her up and into a car seat carrier. I would need to install it into the taxi that would meet us on the street outside.

"Okay, Bunny, let's just slide you into position and clip you in." I heard the clicks of the harness as it buckled Alice safely into the car seat carrier. I just needed to bring the base along with me for the cab, and then we were all set to go.

As I walked toward the front door, I remembered another essential item I would need to bring along with me: the stack of cash I had been slowly gathering. I had managed to save over five thousand in notes. Michael always left me too much money each week for things like groceries and nappies. He seemed to have no idea what anything cost anymore, and would often give me a small fortune in cash. I had scrimped and saved on items where I could, to slowly build up the reserves I'd need to leave him.

I had only recently decided to take Alice and go, but I'd been hiding the money away the entire time. Did part of me know things wouldn't work out between us, that he'd try to take Alice from me? It was sickening to realize I'd always known things would fall apart, that I'd have no choice but to take Alice and never look back.

Michael had given me no alternative. His behavior over the past six months only served to make me think the worst of him. It was like he could not forgive me for the emergency birth. He hated me for being so stressed out that I caused Alice to be born early. It wasn't my fault, but he failed to understand that. Now he was driving me to the point of no return by convincing me that he was going to steal Alice away from my protection, like I wasn't a good mother. Well, I had plans of my own that day. No one was going to take my Bunny without a fight.

With the money secured and everything packed that Alice and I would need for the next few days, I picked up the carrier, our luggage, and the base. If anyone asked what I was up to, I would tell them that we were visiting my mother for a day out of town. It wasn't far from the truth. I would eventually need to see my parents for support. Just not right away.

I shuffled toward the door, encumbered with more items than I could easily carry. Before I reached the door handle, it jiggled and opened as the electromagnetic lock disengaged. I almost dropped everything when I saw Michael standing in the doorframe. Confusion spread across his face as he stared at me; the door swung slowly open with a slight creak.

"What are you doing?" he whispered.

I stood, frozen. I couldn't say a word. I had no excuses or reasons for the sight before him. I was about to leave the apartment with several of my belongings and our only child, without any explanation.

"Nothing," I said. "What are you doing?"

Michael cleared his throat. "I forgot one of my reports for a client, so I came back to the apartment to grab it. What the hell is going on, Erika?"

I relaxed my shoulders and put everything down carefully. I unclipped Alice and lifted her out of the carrier seat. I held her tight against my body and gently patted her back.

"Well?" he pressed.

With a heavy sigh, I closed my eyes for a moment to think. When I opened them back up, Michael had moved a step closer. "What do you think I'm doing?" I asked.

He crossed his arms over his chest. "It looks like you're leaving… forever."

"Well then, no need to keep guessing, is there?"

"God," he said, as both hands landed on his forehead. "Why now? After everything we've—"

"You know exactly why, Michael. Don't lie to me. I can take everything else, it's the lying that I can't stand."

"What are you talking about?" he asked with wide eyes.

I saw right through his facade and saw the BS he was spinning me. His training as a lawyer had made the lies from his mouth damn near impossible to detect, but I'd known Michael long enough to recognize what he was trying to do. There was little point in arguing with him.

"Let's not do this," I said. "We're past it. We've been past it for a while now. Just do the right thing and accept you can't take her from me. Let us go."

Michael stared at me and glanced at Alice. I could see his face change when his eyes found her. He didn't move them from that position until I spoke again.

"Are you going to let us leave?" I asked.

He snapped out of his trance. "Leave? Where exactly are you going?"

"That's none of your concern."

"Oh, I think you'll find that it is," he snapped.

"Don't raise your voice to me, or I'll call the police."

"And what?" Michael asked. "You'll tell them I hit you? Tell them I'm a danger to be around?"

"I wouldn't need to stoop to that level. They'd just have to spend five minutes alone with you to see what a terrible person you are."

I saw Michael's nostrils flare as he breathed heavily and took another step toward us.

"Don't come any closer," I said. Alice started to wail, unhappy with the tone of our voices. I looked down at her and tried to provide comfort. "Look what you've done now. She's upset."

Michael took another step. "You can't do this," he said.

I tried to calm Alice, but she wouldn't quiet down. "There, there, Bunny. It's okay. Time to be quiet."

Michael didn't respond. Instead, he held the bridge of his nose between his thumb and index finger as his other hand stayed firmly across his chest, gripping his elbow.

I continued to speak to Alice and finally saw some progress. She stopped crying and eased off enough for me to put her back into her carrier so I could begin to load up.

"You're still going? Why?"

I grabbed the last bag with difficulty and shook my head at him. "We have to go. Now, are you going to let me past?"

The question hung in the air for a moment. Michael stared at me, his eyes burning. "I thought we could work things out. I thought things might change."

I came as close to Michael as I was comfortable doing. "There was a time when I thought that was possible too, but we went past it. Now please, step aside."

Without another sound, he stepped away from the front door and gestured for us to leave, without taking his eyes off mine. We stepped on through to the corridor. I turned back to see him still facing me.

Michael let us walk right by him and out of his life. What took me so long?

CHAPTER 35

Now

"Which apartment do you think he might be hiding in?" I quietly ask Gus, as we stay hidden at the far end of the seventh floor. The police would be arriving at the building and possibly coming up to Mrs. Stellar's apartment within the next ten minutes, according to Gus's estimate.

"Hard to say. He's got a lot to choose from, but a few options stick out to me. Our key cards can open practically any door in the building. The only thing we have to worry about is justifying why we would open a certain door, as every swipe is recorded against each card. Desmond has his own card, as do I. Every thirty days, our company audits the key card history against resident requests for maintenance. But I doubt Desmond plans on hanging around long enough to be caught by some audit."

"Is it possible to see where he has been right now?"

"Not from here. The records can be accessed by the company we work for and handed over to the police."

"So we can only guess where he might be." I lower my head as a realization comes to me. "He's probably got someone else's card, anyway."

"If he's smart enough to cover his bases, yes. I'd imagine it was the first thing he thought of."

"Great. So my little girl's chances of being found slip away while Desmond remains safely hidden."

Gus shakes his head. "Not if I can help it. There are some things I can forgive in this world, but taking a child from their parent is not one of them."

I raise my head and give Gus the best smile I can manage, given how tired and worn down I am feeling. Coming so close to Alice only to lose her again has taken a toll on me I never imagined possible. I have to find her, and fast, before Desmond tries to flee the building, past Henry's lockdown.

"If you were in his position, where would you go on this floor?"

Gus scratches at his chin. There's a thin layer of stubble forming. "If I wanted an apartment that would be good to hide in, I'd have to go with 701. It's close to the elevator, is fully furnished, and all of its utilities are on, because it's technically being rented but the tenant never uses the place. Some of the guys are known to create false maintenance calls so they can take breaks in there from time to time when things get quiet."

I shake my head. "Well, it's a good start. Only one problem."

"What's that?"

"The police are about to arrive, and Mrs. Stellar is still stalking the hallways. Her apartment is fairly close to 701, isn't it?"

Gus leans out, checking the corridor for the old crone. "If she's standing out the front of her door, it's very close. Knowing her, she will be hanging out at the entrance of her apartment or will have left her door wide open. I'll head back to Mrs. Stellar and distract the old dear. I'll see if I can get her to go back inside and stay in her apartment before the police get here."

"That might take a while. What if I check out 701 while you keep her busy?"

Gus shakes his head. "If Desmond is in there with Alice, he'll be backed into a corner. You'll need all the help you can get to save your little girl without any risk of him hurting her—or you."

I let out a groan. He's right. If I rush in and catch Desmond off guard, he might freak out and think it's all over. A desperate man in that position might be capable of any number of actions. I couldn't live with myself if I caused Alice any harm as a result of my impatience.

"I guess I have no other option but to wait then."

Gus nods as he begins to walk away from me. "I'll move as fast as I can. Unfortunately, Mrs. Stellar can be a real pain in the ass."

"You don't need to tell me." I can still feel the pain in my wrists from her unexpected handcuffing. I take a peek down the hallway as Gus leaves, and hope that we aren't too late to find Desmond. It seems crazy that he's still in the building. Michael must have really needed him and Alice close by for his plan to work. I wonder when he's planning on showing himself. Is he waiting for the whole day to go by so he will have a substantial alibi established at work?

I push the idea out of my head. The planning and execution of a kidnapping is not something I want to ponder. How Michael managed to go through with this makes me want to vomit. Did he not understand the lasting impact this experience would have on her for the rest of her life?

For a solid two years, he seemed to give up on the idea of taking Alice from me. It wasn't until she turned three that he tried to get more involved in her life again, with requests for more visits. When those got denied, he would show up unannounced and try to spend more time with his daughter. Had he realized that Alice was a person who'd one day grow up and understand the truth about her father?

Whatever the reason, it didn't matter. I would never let him take her from me. Not while I was still breathing.

CHAPTER 36

I stand behind a support column in the corridor, tucked just around the corner from the area of the seventh floor where three things exist: Mrs. Stellar, apartment 701, and the elevator.

Gus approaches Mrs. Stellar's apartment, making it appear as if he has come back from chasing me around the building. I can hear the concerned old woman out in the hall, still complaining, hoping the whole world acknowledges her.

I can just picture the frustration on Mrs. Stellar's face when she finds out that Gus has failed to apprehend me. The old crone will moan and sneer at him, unimpressed with any effort he has made. Gus will need to smile and nod to speed things along, trying to get her back inside. I don't envy him.

"Mrs. Stellar," I hear Gus say in the distance.

"Where is she? The police will be here soon."

"That's probably a good thing," he says, "because she gave me the slip."

"Of course she did," she says with a tut. "I knew I should have chased after her myself. I always say you're better off doing things yourself."

I shake my head. Mrs. Stellar couldn't keep up with a runaway shopping cart, let alone a woman my age. She did seem to be the expert when it came to taking down people using handcuffs, though. There was something about being restrained by an old lady and fastened to a radiator that seemed outright insane. But this day was proving to be nothing but a big mess of crazy.

"If the police are almost here, then you should head back inside your apartment. We don't want anything bad happening, do we?"

"Nonsense. I'll be fine right where I am, thank you. That girl is no match for me, and anyway, Henry is going to call me when the police arrive."

She must have filled Henry in on the call she placed to the police. Hopefully, it didn't take long for him to realize who it was that Mrs. Stellar had placed in handcuffs. As soon as the police arrive, he will tell them the rest of the story and paint me in the right light. Thank God I have a few people on my side who believe in me.

I listen while Gus continues to struggle with Mrs. Stellar. She refuses to budge from her position in the corridor, which gives her a clear view of the apartment we need to check. I decide I can't wait much longer for this situation to resolve itself. I have to check out apartment 701. Too much time has been wasted; time that Alice does not have to lose. At any moment, Desmond could work out just how screwed he really is and run. I creep further along, until I'm at the edge of the hallway.

As carefully as I possibly can be, I inch my head around the corner and take a peek at Gus and Mrs. Stellar. She is still outside of her apartment, arguing, but Gus has her distracted. He nods away and listens to her ranting and raving about a completely irrelevant topic to her current predicament. I feel like he deserves a medal for his efforts. I would have lost it by now.

I spot apartment 701 on the other side of the elevator to where I am and glance down at Henry's key card, which I still have in my possession. I'm so glad Henry is now on my side along with Gus. The head of maintenance could have easily seen me as a nothing but a liar and escorted me off the premises. I guess him temporarily losing his own child in the park a few years ago gave him enough perspective to want to be the kind of person who helps a parent in need instead of looking in the opposite direction.

I pull out the card and inspect the piece of plastic. It amazes me that Henry can easily access any home within the building with a quick swipe. I assume Henry's card is held to the same level of scrutiny as the maintenance workers'.

Seeing Mrs. Stellar with her back facing my direction gives me enough confidence to creep into the main corridor and move down to the next support column. Gus sees my move and locks his gaze on the old lady, so she doesn't suspect I'm behind her, sneaking around.

"I suppose I could go back inside and leave my door open," Mrs. Stellar says. A moment later, she and Gus are walking into her apartment.

I move again while the opportunity still exists, and see the hesitation and concern lining Gus's face as he steps inside. He is not comfortable with my impromptu idea to go and open up 701 on my own. I know myself that it's a terrible idea, but I can't wait another second. If Alice is in there, she needs me. She needs her mommy to rescue her from the awful people who thought it would be okay to take a young girl from her mother in broad daylight.

I reach Mrs. Stellar's apartment and dash past, catching a glimpse of Gus looking back out the door.

"What are you looking at?" Mrs. Stellar asks Gus. I duck behind the nearest support column.

"Nothing," he says.

"No, it's something. I saw your eyes twitching about. Did you see someone out in the hallway? I'd better check it out."

Crap. What is with this crazy old bat? Either she thinks I'm not a threat in the slightest or she wants to be the hero of the building.

"There's nothing there," Gus says, trying to stop her. I can hear her footsteps shuffling in my direction. I'm trapped where I stand. Across the way from me is apartment 701.

"There has to be something catching your eye," Mrs. Stellar says. "It could be that girl again, back for more."

I press myself tighter and tighter against the wall, somehow hoping I can turn invisible before the old lady sees me. I don't know how I'll be able to weasel my way out of this one without compromising Gus's job. I don't want him to be fired because he made the mistake of helping me out. He doesn't deserve it.

The elevator beeps a sharp note, startling me. The doors roll open and I hear two lots of footsteps come out.

"About time you showed up," Mrs. Stellar says.

I can't see who she's talking to, but I think I can guess quite easily.

"Mrs. Stellar, I presume. My name is Officer Mason of the NYPD. We are responding to a kidnapping call made earlier. Apparently, a little girl has been taken. Henry here tells me that you had a woman handcuffed inside your apartment, but she managed to escape? Do you know where she might be? We need to talk to her as soon as possible."

I don't know if the police officer is on my side or not, but Henry is standing right next to him. He has to have told the man everything he needs to know about me. Gus hasn't said a word, so I step out from hiding.

"I'm here."

"That's her," Mrs. Stellar yells, pointing a shaky finger at me.

"Just take it easy, Mrs. Stellar," Gus says, as he ushers the old lady back into her apartment.

"But that's her. She's the one harassing poor Desmond. Arrest her, Officer."

Gus continues to deal with Mrs. Stellar for me.

"Erika," Henry says, "are you okay?"

"I'm fine, Henry," I say with a nod. I snap my focus to Officer Mason. "Officer, my daughter has been kidnapped by a maintenance man in this building. I think he's on this floor right now with my little girl, specifically in this apartment here, 701."

"Okay, ma'am. Why don't you take a step back from that door until my backup arrives? I'm the first officer to respond, but more will be here any minute now to search the building for your little girl."

"Can we look in this apartment now? She's in there." I know in my heart she is in there. I can almost feel her pulse beating through the walls. I walk closer to the door. Mason rushes toward me, but he is a good few paces away.

A second before I reach the entry, the door bursts inward. A gust of air tugs at me and I feel a jolt down my spine as I see Desmond standing in the doorway, looking just as stunned as I am.

CHAPTER 37

Desmond and I stop and stare at each other for a fleeting moment, both waiting for the other to make a move. I see a streak of sweat dotting his brow; he has been busy all this time, running around kidnapping my child on Michael's behalf. It takes all of my restraint not to attack him. I can't see Alice.

"Sir," Officer Mason yells. "Stay right where you are. Do not move."

Desmond clutches the door so tight his knuckles begin to turn white as he glances from me to the police officer. I knew I'd be putting myself in harm's way by confronting Desmond, but the reality and danger of the situation doesn't hit me until now.

"Get down on the ground," the officer orders, as he pulls out his pistol.

Desmond doesn't move an inch.

"Where is she?" I ask, my voice almost breaking as I battle my fear. My question sparks a chuckle from Desmond, though I can't begin to fathom its meaning. What has he done?

"Desmond!" Gus yells out from behind. My eyes snap to Gus's in an instant; he is standing in the corridor beside Officer Mason. Before I know it, I am being pushed out of the way by Desmond, with a swift shove that sends me flying back. I hit my head on the wall—hard.

A sense of empty peace overtakes my mind as I slowly fade out, my eyes rolling into the back of my head.

*

I know I'm dreaming when I find myself walking through empty city streets in a summer dress. The outfit ripples slowly in the breeze, as if I'm underwater. I'm walking down the middle of Times Square, surrounded by all of the billboards and lights, but seeing only one image on the many screens: Alice's face. Despite being aware of the off-color cityscape around me, I can't escape this reality.

"Alice," I call up to the electronic billboards, as my daughter gazes down upon me from every direction. She has dirt on her face and her hair is a mess.

"Mommy?" she asks.

"I'm here, Bunny. Where are you?"

"I'm right in front of you, Mommy. Can't you see me?"

Every single image of Alice disappears in a blink. The light of the street beams down at my stomach. It has swollen up again, as if I'm pregnant. I begin instinctively to rub my belly over the silk of the flowing summer dress. I feel the kick of my child in the womb.

"Alice?" I ask her.

"I'm here, Mommy."

"No, that isn't right. You—" I don't finish my thought, as my belly shrinks back down while Alice materializes a few steps in front of me.

"I'm here, Mommy," she says again.

I move toward her and see her vanish with a puff of smoke. She reappears fifty feet away, further into Times Square.

"What are you doing, Bunny? You shouldn't be out here. It's dangerous." I suddenly see scores of vehicles filling the streets. The empty roads are now crammed with taxis, cars, and trucks, their drivers going about their busy days.

"Alice. Stop right now."

"No, Mommy. Daddy's here. He's going to save me."

"No, he won't," I say. "He's not here to save you, Bunny; he's here to take you from me."

"That's a horrible thing to say," Michael says, as his face shows up on every screen in Times Square. I stare up at the billboards, seeing that they span in all directions.

"Give her back!" I yell.

Michael laughs wildly, like a maniac. "I never took her, Erika. You did. You lost our daughter."

"I didn't mean to let her out of my sight. She got out through the elevator. It wasn't my fault."

"It's never your fault, is it? Erika is always the victim. Everyone else is wrong, aren't they?"

"No, it's not like that." I close my eyes, trying to leave this world. I can't seem to shake the booming voice Michael sends down from all angles. He laughs again, overwhelming my senses with flashing lights as a violent storm begins to pour down to drown me like a rat. I feel the water rising.

"Alice," I yell over the laughter, over the rain, over the pain of my existence. "Bunny, come back to me. I need you."

The water doesn't stop filling the streets. An oversize wave comes crashing through the city, spilling across every surface, rolling cars and debris along its deadly path.

I can't stop the inevitable. Death is about to claim me.

*

A splash of water hits my face and wakes me up. I rub the liquid out of my eyes and see Gus standing over me with an empty glass. It doesn't take long for me to work out where the water came from.

"Are you okay?" Gus asks me.

I scratch my head. "Yeah, I guess."

"Let me take a look. I'm just going to lean your body forward to check if there's any blood coming from the back of your head."

I comply and let him inspect me. He finds nothing to fret about. A flood of memories all hit me at once as I remember Desmond shoving me firmly into the wall. "Alice," I blurt out.

"She's not in there. He's hidden her somewhere else. But don't worry. Officer Mason is looking for Desmond as we speak. He chased him up the stairs. As soon as he apprehends the bastard, he'll tell us where Alice is."

"How do you know? What if Desmond's already hurt her—or worse? What if Mason has to shoot him and he never gets a chance to tell us?"

Gus hold up his hands. "Hey, calm down, okay? The police will find Desmond. Desmond will give up Alice. Trust me."

I feel my lungs working overtime to take in tiny breaths of air and expel them just as quickly. How can he be so sure? How can he possibly know everything will be okay? I start to remember that Henry and Mrs. Stellar were around when Desmond shoved me over.

"What about the old lady and Henry?"

"Taken care of. Officer Mason sent her back inside with instructions not to come out until it is safe to do so. Henry went with Mason after Desmond."

"God," I say, as I slump back against the wall Gus has me leaning on. A lot happened while I was out of it.

"You just need to take it easy for a few minutes. You might have a concussion."

I ignore his words and start to stand up.

"Erika, what did I just tell you?"

I wave him off. "I'm not going to sit around here all day. We have to find her right now." I brush myself off.

He shakes his head at me. "Nothing's going to stop you, is it?"

I turn back to face him fully again. "I don't have a choice. I have to save her."

CHAPTER 38

Then

Six months had passed since I'd left Michael. Alice and I had had our share of tough moments during that time. Michael came after me the next day with the police. They found us at a cheap hotel out of the city, but to Michael's disgust, they couldn't force me to come home. Instead, they moved me into some temporary housing until I found something better. Alice was being taken care of, so the matter of custody would have to be settled in court.

When the judge said Michael could only visit once every two weeks, he lost it in court and had to be restrained. I tried to use that outburst to take away his biweekly visit, but Michael calmed down and apologized to the judge.

I filed for a divorce as soon as I could, and Michael didn't fight me on the decision. I reverted to my maiden name while I waited for the slow divorce procedure to go through, and Michael offered to give me money each week for Alice's care before child support was demanded of him. He still thought he could influence her care from a distance. Despite my fears, he seemed to be doing the right thing for us all. I only hoped it would last and he wouldn't try to force us back home.

I didn't want to rely on Michael's money forever, so I knew I would need to return to working part-time to keep giving Alice what she needed. This meant I would need to enroll her in daycare.

Before I found the right facility for my Bunny, I tried out a few places around my area that were within my budget. Once I found a job, I would need to put her in daycare three days per week, at the young age of only twelve months. It killed me to be away from her, but I had no choice. Michael's child support had served me well, but I wanted to eventually break away from that dependence.

I decided I'd rather return to admin work to make enough extra money to provide Alice with what she deserved. While I was trying to secure a job and a place for Alice, I was forced to rely on my neighbor to look after my Bunny so I could scout out an appropriate center.

I came across a reasonable facility, only a ten-minute bus ride from my new apartment, which was way out of the city. It was nothing like the building she should have gone to in Brooklyn Heights, but those days were gone, with no chance of ever coming back.

I had scheduled a tour with one of the managers at a center called Moorhall Family Daycare. It was bigger than the daycare in Brooklyn Heights, in a purpose-built building. I shook the manager's hand as she welcomed me into the reception area.

"Hello, Miss Rice. My name is Vina Schwartz. I am the manager here on Mondays to Wednesdays."

"Pleased to meet you," I said, looking at the tall brunette and taking in her demeanor. She appeared to be in her late thirties and was wearing simple clothing—essential for wrangling dozens of children at once.

"I suppose you're dying to see the place. Shall we begin?"

I nodded. "Yes, please."

We moved through a security door at the front of the building, designed to prevent children from escaping. I guessed it was also to prevent anyone from taking them, but that was a scenario I never imagined possible.

"This is where Alice would take a nap if you decide to go with us," Vina said. I gazed out at a sea of cots and toddler beds all crammed in together. As cute as they looked, I felt a pit in my stomach at the thought of Alice trying to take her nap in such a busy environment. What if she couldn't fall asleep? Would her development be stunted as a result? Would her nighttime sleep be ruined? Dozens of questions entered my mind as I was shown to the next area.

"And here we have one of the play areas designated for children aged twelve months to three years. We have one staff member per four children. Alice will spend her first few years in this room before she moves on up to the next area."

I gazed around at the room, which was well worn but obviously cared for. There were fun activities and educational toys for Alice to play with. I couldn't fault any one thing about the space, other than the fact that Alice would be spending the next two years here, three days a week.

I stumbled back and out of the room. Fortunately, we were moving quickly along on the tour. I was shown where the kids would eat and go to the toilet, as well as outside to see a few of the playgrounds reserved for different age groups.

It was a beautiful facility, and the staff seemed warm and inviting. I really had no choice but to put Moorhall Family Daycare down as one of my top picks. This meant handing over a non-refundable deposit to secure a place, whether I selected the facility or not.

Vina took me back to the reception area to start the process. I had arranged the tour over the phone and had yet to give them my full details and credit card information.

"Okay, let's get this underway," Vina said. I gave her every detail needed to secure Alice a place within the next few weeks. The price was a little higher than the two other daycares I'd applied to, but it seemed to be worth the extra expense.

"Alright. Now I just need to send this off to our system at HQ, and we'll be all set." Vina made a show of hitting the send button. Working with children as much as she did probably caused her to talk in an overenthusiastic way.

Vina's brows tightened as she leaned in closer to the screen. "That doesn't seem right," she said. "I'll try again." I heard her click a few buttons as she concentrated entirely too hard on the problem. "Oh."

"Oh?" I asked. "What's wrong?"

Vina cleared her throat. Her forehead wrinkled as she moved her hand to her lips. Something was not right.

"It appears to be some sort of automated response that won't allow me to sign you up. This is quite odd. I've never seen anything like this before."

"Okay," I said, unsure what to make of her comment.

"Tell you what," Vina said, "why don't you take a seat in our waiting room while I get this sorted with the director. I'm probably doing something wrong. But rest assured, Bernetta always knows the answer to these problems." Vina smiled at me, but I saw her face drop the second she began to turn away from me. What was going on?

I tried to remain calm as I walked out to the small waiting room near the reception area, where parents would wait for their children at the end of the day. It was another security measure the facility had in place.

Why wasn't their system allowing me to register? And why did Vina's face drop? Something had given her reason to go straight to the director of the place. It didn't make sense.

I stared at the ground and bounced my legs up and down on the spot. I closed my eyes for a moment and tried to block out the building anxiety I was prone to suffering from. If I didn't calm down, it would push me over the edge.

I kicked off my shoes and clenched my toes. I focused on my breathing as best I could, wishing I had a paper bag. After a few minutes, I began to calm down. Whatever the problem was, I would face it. I'd come this far on my own. Nothing could stop me now.

Vina came back with who I assumed was Bernetta. I quickly put my shoes back on.

Vina stared at me for a moment. "Unfortunately, Erika, we won't be able to offer you a place here. I'm sorry."

"Why? What seems to be the problem?" I asked, as my eyes flicked between the two.

They shared a quick look. "I'm sorry," said Bernetta, "but we can't help you."

"What? Clearly, this is some sort of mistake, right?"

"We're sorry, our system miscalculated, and we are actually fully booked."

"Fully booked?"

"I'm afraid so," Bernetta said. "Now, is there anyone we can call for you?"

I stared around at the other staff members in the reception area. A lone parent was also nearby, waiting for their child. I felt a sting of embarrassment smack me in the face. Why was this happening? What had I done to be denied a place so quickly, and why were they asking if there was anyone they could call for me? The answer hit me a second later. How could I not see it?

"This is because of my ex-husband, Michael, isn't it?"

Bernetta's eyes betrayed her the second I said Michael's name. She exchanged a look with Vina. "Why don't I give him a call. He can come pick you up."

"You can't be serious? I'm not going anywhere with him." I didn't realize at first, but I had risen to my feet. This caused the two daycare workers to back up a step.

"That's fine, but you will need to leave," Bernetta said.

"Leave? I'm not doing anything wrong!" My voice was rising, but I couldn't help myself. What had Michael told these people about me?

Bernetta and Vina backed away and gestured toward the exit. I flicked my eyes from one person to the next while my nostrils flared in and out with my breath. "This is some sort of mistake. It has to be. I'm just trying to find an adequate daycare center for my Bunny."

"We understand, Erika, but we can't help you. Please leave right now, before this situation gets out of hand."

"Out of hand? What exactly do you think I'm going to do?" I asked, as I threw both of my hands up into the air. The waiting parent to my side didn't move a muscle, as if they were hoping to not draw any attention to themselves.

"We can discuss this further outside, if you'd like?"

"No," I said, as I shook my head. I wrapped both hands around my face. Had Michael really gone to this much effort to control where I enrolled Alice? I knew his money had power, but I never realized until then that he could influence and control my life from afar like this. I had no choice but to leave.

"I'm leaving." It took everything I had not to unload my every frustration on these people, but I realized it was not going to help in any way. I had to go.

"Right this way," Bernetta said. She gestured toward the set of double doors at the front of the reception area. I moved along a few steps and kept my eyes down and forward. I couldn't help the next words out of my mouth.

I turned my head toward them both and said, "You will be hearing from me about this." I hit an exit button and walked through the double doors as they opened to the parking lot. I didn't dare look back at the many people who would be watching my every move.

How could Michael be so cruel? I realized at that moment that this wasn't the first daycare center to reject my application. Two other facilities had given me excuses about capacity issues that I had believed to be true at the time. It was obvious now that it was all BS.

Michael was out there, making it impossible for me to get the care Alice needed so that I could work. Was this all part of his plan to force us back home? Or was he slowly building toward something far worse?

CHAPTER 39

Now

I decide to search through the apartment Desmond has been hiding in, despite what Gus has to say on the matter. Officer Mason is still in pursuit of Desmond. I can't wait for any other officers to arrive and be filled in on the situation. Alice needs me now.

I try to work out if Alice has been in here with him. There are no toys or pieces of paper with colorful drawings on them. There's no mess and no bits of food left out.

I can't smell any traces of her in any of the rooms. My daughter's clothing emanates a particular scent from the laundry powder I've used ever since she was born. Every time I catch a whiff of her fragrance, my mind flies back to her days as a baby rolling around on the floor, still trying to figure out what the world around her was all about.

I don't know if we ever truly understand the world we live in, especially some of the people that occupy it. How can there be so many monsters hiding in plain sight, like Michael and his recruited team? I shudder at the thought that Alice had been forced to share a space with Desmond for several hours. She didn't deserve to be boxed in with a freak like that.

"She's not here," Gus says.

"I know. I'm just trying to work out if she ever was."

"What do you mean? Do you think he hid her somewhere else?"

I turn to Gus. "It's possible. Explains why he took off on his own."

Gus walks further around with one hand on his forehead. "This is getting messy. So where did he hide her then?"

"She can't be far. The location has to be on this floor. We were hot on his tail. We both saw her with him. It has to be one of these apartments. He could have put her in any one of the empty ones, using his key cards."

Gus stares at me in agreement, then his gaze becomes distant, as if a thought has claimed him.

"What is it?"

He blinks. "It's probably nothing."

"Tell me. Please?" I step closer and give him a pathetic face, full of desperation.

He scratches the back of his head and shifts on the spot. "Okay, there's one possibility we haven't considered yet."

"Which is?"

"What if he sent her down the stairwell? We assumed he was headed for this floor with her. What if he sent her off on her own?"

I let the possibility run through my head. Alice would keep going until she hit the ground floor. She would head out into the lobby. Henry was up here with Mason. What if she found it empty, with no adults around? No one would be there to help her. What would she do then?

I stare back at Gus and shake my head. "He wouldn't do that. It would put her in danger. Michael doesn't want his daughter hurt. He just wants her taken away from me. He has for some time now. I hate to admit that, but it's true. During a recent visit, I could tell he left with a plot hatching in his brain. I didn't realize that it was to remove Alice from my custody."

"Wow," Gus says. "And I thought some of the people I know are messed up."

"Yep. So she has to be close. He would have locked her in an apartment to keep her both safe and away from me."

Gus crosses his arms and stares around the living room. A fine layer of dust coats every surface, except for the coffee table, which Desmond and his co-workers sometimes use. I wonder if Gus is one of those people that abuses the trust of the residents. Is he another corrupt individual that thinks they are above the rules? I think not.

"I guess we'd better start searching for her then," Gus said. "As you say, she can't be far. We should start with the empty apartments. I doubt he would pick one that has anyone living in it."

"Hopefully not," I say. "I can't deal with another old woman handcuffing me to a radiator."

Gus chuckles. I return his positivity as best I can. Alice is close by. I can feel it. This apartment seems to radiate her location to me. I can tell in my heart she is near. I can't seem to shake the feeling that this is where she is.

"Come on," Gus says. "Let's save your daughter." He heads for the door. I follow him, semi-reluctant to budge from the spot. It feels stupid to think that I can sense her location like I have superpowers, but I can't ignore her presence. Still, I obey and go along with Gus.

We search the empty apartments, starting with the ones furthest away from the elevator. It seems unlikely that Desmond would have reached any of them and then had enough time to run back to the apartment he chose to hide in, but we need to eliminate the possibility in case Alice escaped on her own.

Each apartment is the same: empty spaces and their mirrored equivalents. I see the same layouts over and over, driving me to wonder how anyone can have an identity in this building, or in any other of the giant apartment complexes that exist in the neighborhood.

I am reminded of the awful task of finding Alice and me a place to live, after Michael gave us no choice but to leave, six months into her life. We searched for somewhere to live without knowing what our budget would be. Michael had taken it upon himself to remove me from the workforce, trying to limit my ability to leave him. It didn't stop me, though. I was so glad I had squirreled away five thousand in cash to help get us started. I got out with Alice before anything could happen to her. But now Michael has started what he never had the guts to do back then, and Alice is in danger.

I remember the tiny one-bedroom apartments with their paper-thin walls and odd smells. As soon as I realized that living closer to the city would cost me more, I decided to move Alice and I further out, until I found the perfect community. It would make visits with Michael harder than they needed to be, but at least I could manage our finances until I could gain employment.

"Alice? You in there, sweetie?" Gus was putting on his best voice for a little girl to respond to. My only worry was that Alice had come across too many people today. "Nothing in this one," he said.

We were too far away from where I had felt the connection to Alice. None of these empty apartments would hold her. She had to be in something that was near 701. I just knew it.

"Okay. These are all occupied," Gus said, "but the next few are empty."

I stopped him with a single hand on his bicep as I felt a twitch of pain hit my head. "She's not in any of them."

"What do you mean?"

"I can't explain it, but I could feel her. I sensed her before, when we were in 701. She's somewhere near there, I just know it." I shake my head as I close my eyes. I must sound insane.

"Where do you think she might be?" Gus asks. "Apart from Mrs. Stellar's apartment, they are all taken in that area. All that's left is Desmond's apartment. But surely he wouldn't go there?"

It hits me like a wall of bricks. "No, he wouldn't, but there's one other apartment close by with no one in it."

Gus's mouth falls open as he waits to hear what I have to say. "Which one?"

I almost kick myself for not trying it to begin with. I stare at Gus. "Alan's."

CHAPTER 40

I stand outside Alan's apartment while Gus readies his key card for access. I can feel Alice's presence stronger than ever. It pains me to think that we didn't try this door before any others. Desmond would have been desperate when we were on his tail. It wasn't the best hiding place, but it was still a location that could contain a child.

I take in a deep breath and exhale as the door unlocks when Gus swipes his card. I know she's inside. I've never been so sure of anything in my life.

"Are you okay?" Gus asks me, before I take a single step forward. I turn to him with a tight smile. "I will be."

He returns my smile with a nod. I take a step forward but he grabs my shoulder. "Are you sure you don't want to wait for more police to arrive? We don't know what we're going to find in there."

I place a hand on top of his as I shake my head. "I have to do this, no matter what's in there, okay?"

He steps aside. I shake off the twisted thoughts that have entered my mind because of his caution and move inside Alan's apartment. Now isn't the time to let my imagination take control and think up the worst possibilities.

It seems different as I stroll inside—bigger without all those people cramming it. I feel like I'm seeing it for the first time. My gaze flicks to the dining and kitchen area, and to the mess I made tearing the place apart. Alan's life is laid out for the world to see. Years of existence fill the space in the form of framed photographs and memorabilia. Every part of Alan's history is spread out on display. I see the clubs he belongs to, his love of fishing, his obsession with American muscle cars, his medical bills.

This last item brings me to a stop. Is that why he agreed to help Michael? For a payday he so sorely needed? I think about Desmond, and how Alan might have pressured him into helping out his old man in a time of need. I could imagine the conversation. Alan could have used any number of lines. "I've given you a job and a place to live. You owe me." Could a father really sink that low? But I know it is possible. Today has shown me just that.

I push aside Alan's life and continue past the living space to the single bedroom that finishes off the small apartment. I come to a closed door and pause. My hand begins to shake as I reach for the knob. I grab hold of my wrist and steady it with a deep breath in and out. Now is not the time for this.

"Erika?" Gus asks from behind.

"I'm fine," I say without looking back. "I just need a second."

He doesn't respond as I glance down and reach for the knob again. I grab hold and twist it slowly, not wanting to disturb or scare Alice. The door gently swings open, making the smallest creak as it reaches the wall inside.

The double bed is tucked away to the side, maximizing the space. Alan has drawn the blackout curtains closed, throwing the room into deep darkness, enough for the lightest of sleepers to get some shut-eye. I step inside and see a figure in the bed.

I drop to my knees as I carefully approach her. The figure is small, matching Alice's size. It has to be her. I know in my soul that my Bunny is here before me, waiting to be saved.

Is she alive?

Only time will tell what fate has in store.

She is asleep on her side. I see the tiny rise and fall of her chest and belly and know that she's breathing. Her long hair half covers her face, so I brush it gently aside and smile down upon Alice's innocent features.

Gus stands in the doorframe. I look up to him and nod as tears fill my eyes. "It's her," I whisper. "She's okay."

He smiles back at me with a few tears of his own. "I told you we'd find her," he says.

"Thank you," is all I can say in return. I face my Bunny again and see her in the deepest sleep of her life. She has no doubt had the worst time ever and will need to sleep for twelve hours straight. I feel the lure of my bed at home, and the fatigue finally hits my brain in the form of a headache.

But I can't rest now. I need to get Alice to a doctor to see if she's okay. I don't know if Desmond had enough brains to keep her safe or not.

I remember that a police officer is currently chasing Desmond through the building as I stare at Alice. All I can hope is that Desmond and Michael both get what's coming to them. Alan had already been punished, as far as I'm concerned.

Alice stirs a little in the bed but remains asleep. Her movement reminds me of what is important—more so than revenge or justice. Michael and Desmond will be caught, one way or the other. Right now, I need to focus on Alice and get her home in one piece.

I gently scoop my hands underneath her body and lift her up. I place her head on my shoulder and pat her hair, making sure she remains asleep. She is so out of it that she doesn't wake up.

I walk toward Gus as he steps back and out of the way. He allows me to leave the apartment first, opting to escort us safely out while the manhunt for Desmond continues.

As we reach the hallway, the police officer comes through from the stairwell door. I turn to face him, seeing sweat covering his forehead. He sees me with Alice and quietly approaches.

"Are you okay, ma'am?"

"Yes, thank you, Officer. We found her in Alan Bracero's apartment. That's Desmond's father." I go on to explain what happened to Alan, and the relationship he and his kidnapper son had in secret within the building. I thought about walking away to focus on Alice, but the words flow freely out of my mouth. The officer needs to know everything. What if Michael tries this again? What if he gets away with today? I go on to tell the officer about Michael and my thoughts on his involvement.

The officer takes it all down without much surprise. Either he has seen this happen before, or something has happened to convince himself I'm telling him the truth.

"Can I ask where Desmond is?"

Officer Mason lets out his breath through his nostrils. "Unconscious and cuffed to a pipe. I was forced to knock him out cold on the roof when I found him. He attempted to attack me with a knife, shouting something about not wanting to go back to prison."

My mouth hangs open. "Oh my God. Are you okay, Officer? Are you hurt?"

"I'm fine, ma'am. More importantly, is your little girl okay? Does she need medical attention?"

"I think she's okay. I just need to take her home. I'll take her to our local doctor for a full checkup and then straight to bed. I just want her to rest after the hell of a few hours we've had."

"Fair enough," Mason says. "Normally, I'd need her checked by an EMT first and to take your statement. Seeing as you've both had a rough day why don't we escort you down to the lobby and call you a cab? We can sort everything out later."

Gus and the officer guide us to the elevator. I shudder at the thought of going inside. I don't want to take it, but I can't carry Alice down seven floors to the ground.

We ride in silence as the elevator falls gently to the bottom of the building without a single shudder. It only proves to me that

Desmond did something to make it stop near level seven, so he could take Alice from me. I keep my eyes closed the entire time.

I shake my head in disgust as I wonder how much it cost Michael to pay for Alice to be kidnapped. What was the life of a child worth to a father who only saw his offspring as a possession? It didn't matter, in the end. The police would catch up with him the second he showed up. If he ever showed up.

The lobby greets us with open arms. I see Henry at the reception desk, speaking with some more police officers. Mason rushes ahead and directs them where they need to go. I imagine the roof will need to be secured along with Alan and Desmond's apartments. Michael's will also be on the list, without a doubt.

Mason comes back to me as his co-workers head toward the elevator. "We've got things covered from here. Some detectives will be around to your home later in the day, as soon as we've processed this mess. They just need to go over your statement for the record."

"That's no problem. I'll write down my address for you."

Mason hands over his notepad and pen. I jot down my details in a hurry, leaning over Alice's shoulder. I still can't remember my phone number, not that it matters. I'll need a new cell to replace my missing one. But I have what is important, what could never be replaced: my daughter.

"You're free to leave," Mason says.

"Thank you, Officer," I say.

"Just doing my job, ma'am." Mason walks toward Henry. I stare at the receptionist and give him a stern look that says everything it needs to. If only he'd called the police sooner, like he promised, things would be different. Gus was the only one who really deserved praise.

The head of maintenance comes to stand by my side. "She's really asleep," he says as he stares at Alice.

"Long day," I say, as the fatigue begins to take hold.

"Mason asked me to call you a cab." Gus pulls out his cell and dials the number. He speaks to a dispatcher and tells me a cab is on its way.

"So, what do you think will happen to Michael, assuming he's behind all of this?" Gus asks.

I stare at the ground. I am struggling to come to grips with what he has done. How could a father stoop so low? After everything we went through together, how could he have thought this was the best thing for Alice? If he had found it in himself to forgive me for her birth, things wouldn't have been this way. All of this pain could have been avoided.

"To be honest, Gus, I don't care. As long as he is out of our lives forever, I'm happy. Sure, we'll struggle without his money to support Alice, but we'll find a way. We always do."

Gus smiles out of the corner of his mouth. "If you ever need anything, you know where to find me."

We sit down near the front of the lobby, waiting for the cab. I listen as Gus tells me about his kids and his wife. It's nice just to sit and hear about a happy family, instead of focusing on the negative life I've been forced to live these past few years.

The cab pulls up amongst all the police cruisers. "That's my ride," I say. Gus helps me up while Alice continues to sleep on my shoulder. I can feel her weight starting to get to me, but we'll be on our way in a moment. The image of home beckons me onward.

As we head for the exit, Alice begins to stir. "Mommy?" she asks, her voice groggy.

"I'm here for you, baby. Go back to sleep."

Alice places her head back down and settles into my shoulder. I turn to Gus and repeat my thanks. He helps me through the exit and sends me on my way with a smile.

I climb into the cab and place Alice in beside me as best I can, so she can keep sleeping. I give the driver our address and ask him to take it extra cautiously. We're not in a rush.

Alice wakes again for a moment. "Where are we going, Mommy?" Her eyes only open a sliver before they close again.

"Back home, Bunny, away from this place."

Alice wrinkles her brow for a moment and snuggles into me, falling back asleep within seconds.

CHAPTER 41

Officer Mason

Officer Mason had his hands full, trying to direct his people in the right direction as more and more personnel showed up to help with the developing crime scene. Parts of the building had to be locked down to cope with the process. The maintenance man named Gus helped wherever he could, while Mason remained in the lobby with the receptionist and a few other officers in case Michael Walls returned home.

"I'm sorry for any trouble I've caused today," said Henry to Mason.

"Don't beat yourself up, kid. You did what you thought was right. Besides, it all worked out in the end. That mother couldn't be stopped. She was a powerful force."

Henry's eyes fell to the floor. "I'll say."

Mason nodded as he scanned the lobby again, making sure the area was secure. He turned back to Henry. "Do you have kids?" he asked.

"No."

"I do. You don't know this until you see their faces for the first time, but you'd do anything to protect them from harm. You'd give up your life if it meant they could live another day longer in this screwed-up world. How any parent could arrange all of this crap today is beyond me. I sure as hell hope this guy hasn't done what he's been accused of."

"It's crazy," Henry said. "I never imagined Mr. Walls would do something like this. He didn't seem the type."

"They never do, kid. They never do."

Mason took a few steps forward and squinted as he saw the man they were speaking of, Michael Walls, casually approaching the building without a care in the world. "Act normal, Henry. He's coming right now. Make sure he has access to the building. We don't want a big scene to unfold on the sidewalk, do we?"

"No, we don't."

Mason signaled to the two officers he had placed by the lobby doors. They got into position and waited for Michael to walk inside. Mason stared at the arrogant man in his expensive-looking suit as he strolled into the building with confidence. He didn't seem to care that the apartment complex was surrounded by police cruisers.

"Got you now, asshole," Mason muttered.

Once Michael was halfway to the reception desk, Mason gave his officers the signal to move in. Mason stepped out in front.

"Mr. Walls. Can I have a minute of your time?"

Michael stopped in his tracks and looked at the officer. "Sure. Is everything okay?"

"That depends," Mason said.

Before Michael could determine what Mason meant, the two officers had surrounded him. They drew their pistols.

"Don't move, or we'll shoot!" one of them yelled. Michael turned around to see two weapons trained on his body. His hands shot up straight into the air. The officers ordered him to interlace his fingers around the back of his head and fall to his knees. They restrained him in moments.

"What is this?" Michael yelled, as Mason came over. "I'm a lawyer. I'll have you all suspended for this."

"I'd advise you to keep a lid on it," Mason said as he squatted down. He proceeded to shout out Michael's Miranda rights on autopilot. Michael didn't want to hear it.

"What is the meaning of this? I demand to know what is going on, right now."

Mason scoffed. "Don't pretend you don't know. Your little scheme to kidnap your daughter has fallen apart. We've got the guy you paid to take her—he's unconscious on the roof. He's under arrest, of course. Not sure if that puts a damper on your plans."

"What are you talking about?"

Mason laughed. "It's a bit late to play the innocent card, my friend. Your ex-wife unraveled your plans. She's got Alice with her now."

"Oh my God," Michael muttered. "You can't be serious? Erika was here?"

"Yes. And I gotta say, next time you try to pull something like this, you might want to do things a little smarter. Your guy got real sloppy."

"No, no, no. This isn't happening."

"Afraid so, pal." Mason started walking away from Michael.

"Officer wait."

Mason stopped. This was the part where the criminal got desperate and offered him a bribe or tried to tell him that it was all a big misunderstanding. But Michael was going to need to do some smooth talking to convince Mason that he was innocent.

"You have to hear me out."

Mason stepped a few paces back toward Michael and kneeled down. "I'm listening."

"Okay. I haven't paid some guy to kidnap anyone. I haven't been hatching a scheme to get past Erika. This is all a huge mistake."

"That's all you've got? I'm going to need to hear more than that. Erika found Alice and has taken her home. Desmond Bracero is up on the roof in handcuffs, unconscious. His father, Alan, is in the hospital with a fractured skull."

"Oh God. This can't be happening. Please tell me this is a big joke."

"No joke, my man. You've been busted. Your life is about to get a whole lot worse from here on out. Let me ask you something real quick, before we haul your ass away: was it worth it?"

Michael shook his head at Mason. "You don't understand, officer. I—"

"I don't understand?" Mason yelled. "Are you kidding me? You paid people to kidnap your little girl and—"

"I don't have a daughter!" Michael screamed, his voice echoing across the lobby.

Mason's eyes popped out wide for a moment as he faltered. "Bullshit. Don't lie to me. You think I was born yesterday? You won't get out of this that easily."

"I don't have a daughter; I don't have any children," Michael said.

"No, that can't be—"

"Erika is unstable," Michael said, cutting Mason off. "Yes, we were married several years ago, but we don't have any kids together. I swear it."

Any smugness disappeared from Mason's face. Surely the man was lying to get out of trouble, but something in his voice said otherwise. Mason almost dropped to his knees when he thought of something vital. "Wait. If you're telling me the truth, and I'm not saying you are, does that mean…?"

"Yes. Erika has taken someone else's kid."

Mason stood on two shaky legs and stumbled back from Michael. "You have to be lying," he said, as the truth hit him like a runaway bus. He lifted his police hat off his head for a moment and rubbed his forehead. "This has to be a joke."

The elevator dinged a second later, grabbing Mason's attention. Another police officer came running toward him with something in his hands.

"Officer Mason, you are going to want to see this," said a young rookie policewoman. She handed over a wallet encased in a crime scene bag. Mason stared at the open wallet in the plastic and saw what had so rattled the policewoman in an instant.

"This can't be right," he said, as he stared at a photo of Desmond hugging the little girl Erika had just taken away. Both had smiles on their faces.

"She's unstable," Michael said from the floor. "She shouldn't have been here."

Mason dropped down to the ground with the wallet. "This isn't your little girl?"

Michael studied the photo and shook his head. "That's Desmond's daughter. He doesn't get to see her very often because of his criminal record. Most people in the building don't know about her or his past. I only knew him from a professional standpoint. I gave Alan advice when Desmond was still in prison. Recently, Alan and his son came to me for some advice regarding custody of Desmond's little girl. He has a few outstanding warrants and is terrified of losing her. He probably got freaked out when you people showed up here."

Mason's mouth hung open. He tried to regain some composure as best he could. He had one burning question begging to be answered. "Why did Erika take her?"

Michael sighed and closed his eyes for a few moments. "It's hard to explain, but a little over four years ago, she was pregnant with our child. She used to live here with me in the building, until something bad happened."

"What do you mean by 'bad'?" Mason asked.

"I mean the kind of thing that changes a person forever. Erika was taking the elevator up to our apartment when she had a panic attack. She stopped the elevator manually and fell into an anxiety spiral. She was eight and a half months pregnant."

Mason stared at Michael, still sprawled on the ground in the handcuffs the officers had placed upon him. Any lawman worthy of his badge could see that Walls was telling the truth. "What happened?"

Michael glanced away for a moment and took in a long gulp of air. He let his breath out slowly, as if to calm his words. "She lost the baby, right there in the elevator. When the doctors arrived, they had to cut her out of Erika by cesarean. I was at work when this all happened. I rushed down to the hospital as soon as I heard and found Erika in a recovery room, holding our dead child." Tears streaked down Michael's face.

Mason felt his mouth fall open. Three other police officers had gathered around and were listening to Michael's every word.

"She named her Alice and told me to come meet my daughter."

None of the officers spoke. Henry stepped forward and managed a few words. "I saw Desmond step out of the elevator with a little girl. Erika convinced me that she was her daughter and that Desmond had taken her. I didn't realize he was her father."

Mason tried to formulate his next question in his mind, but his brain drew a blank. He was speechless.

Michael continued. "I eventually took Erika home from the hospital, once she was ready to leave, but it didn't end there. Erika continued to think our baby was alive. She…"

Mason studied Michael as he trailed off and sobbed into the floor.

"Are you okay?"

Michael ignored the question and pushed on. "I got doctors in to talk to her, but she wouldn't speak to them. I tried to stay home with Erika to help her through what had happened, through what she was suffering with, but my firm was demanding the world from me at the time, and I had huge bills to pay. They didn't care about my personal life. They didn't care about our loss. I came close to losing my job in the end, but after six months of her sickness, Erika took off and refused to come home. I had no choice but to have her committed."

A silence filled the air as the small group of people stared in shock at the restrained man on the ground of the lobby.

"I still love her," Michael said. "I tried to make it work, but she hated me and kept saying I blamed her for the birth, that I couldn't stand to be in the same room as her. She thought I only cared about our baby. The baby that only she could see. It was like deep down she knew the truth, but at the same time she didn't."

The silence in the lobby was deafening. No one dared to speak. They all waited for Michael to continue.

"I pay for her care and treatment. I forced myself to see past her illness, past her delusions, but she changed her last name straight away and filed for divorce. She tried to enroll our dead daughter in daycare facilities and preschools. I had to send them all warnings about her condition."

Mason saw the stunned faces all around the lobby and pulled himself together. "Where is Erika taking Desmond's daughter? She gave me an address."

"Show it to me," Michael said.

Mason held up the note Erika left him. Michael scanned it and closed his eyes. He knew the place.

"Where is it? I need to send several officers there, right now."

Michael met Mason's gaze as he reopened his eyes. "Rocksville Psychiatric Center. I pay a lot of money for them to give her the help she needs. They take her out on day trips every two weeks. She must have escaped somehow and come here. It's out of the city, in the suburbs. Erika has lived there for the last three and a half years."

CHAPTER 42

Then

The elevator came to a stop with a grinding thud. I don't know why I hit the button, but I couldn't face going up to that apartment again to lie around for the rest of the day, rubbing my belly and feeling sorry for myself. I wanted more than anything else in the world to see Michael for lunch and talk about the concerns I had for our growing family.

I knew the end of our relationship was coming. The baby I was close to having wasn't going to turn things around and bring us together like some magical fairy tale. If anything, she was going to drive us further and further apart.

I wasn't trying to blame my unborn child for all of my problems, but when all was said and done, I wasn't prepared for her the way Michael seemed to be.

I paced around the elevator, unsure of what I was doing in the cramped space. I held my hands tight against my skull, pressing in harder than I ever had before, trying to calm my brain from swirling into a panic. It didn't seem to help. I couldn't stop what was coming.

A pain stabbed into my chest as I struggled to get in enough oxygen. I needed to get the elevator up and running again. I pushed the stop button back in with a shaky hand to kick-start the motors into action. But instead of lurching back up the building, the elevator remained motionless. Then the lights overhead clicked off. The dull, red emergency lighting replaced the bright glow.

Dread filled my every thought as the pain in my chest sharpened. Had I just marooned myself inside a darkened elevator while eight and a half months pregnant? I fell back against the wall and clutched at my clothing, my gaze darting from corner to corner. I was trapped in a tomb of my own creation, with no way out.

I fumbled through my bag to find my cell. Some of my makeup fell out along with my keys as I haphazardly rummaged through my belongings to retrieve my phone. I found my cell a moment later and pulled it out. It slipped through my sweaty fingers like it was covered in butter. I watched as it hit the floor of the elevator with a crack. The phone clattered around the hard surface and settled, its screen broken.

I screamed—louder than I'd ever done in the past. Every frustration, every pained word that was dying to explode out of me, filled that yell with power until it flowed down through to my fists. I slammed the ground over and over as I fell to my side and burst into tears. I had finally lost the fight with the breakdown the whole world had seen coming.

I closed my eyes and wept as my head settled into place on my outstretched arm. I lost all control of who or where I was. I didn't try to pick up my phone to call Michael for help. I just lay there, lifeless, as the world spun around me. Nothing could pull me out of that state. Nothing could save me from the end I hadn't seen coming.

But I was wrong.

She saved me that day with a single kick. I felt her tiny foot press against my belly. She pulled me from the dirty floor to grab my cell. She forced me to get up to my feet. The desperate monsters in the back of my head, the ones that wanted me to give up and fall into the depths of the void that surrounded my existence, would have to wait. Alice needed me.

So I did what needed doing. I called for help. I couldn't get the elevator working again, so I waited for people to pry open its doors and save us from the dark.

They came within the hour and forced the doors open. I'll never forget the look on the police officer's face as he shone his flashlight into the elevator.

The paramedics told me I had gone into early labor in the elevator. They said the stress I had been suffering from might have triggered things.

It all happened so fast. I didn't see the blood on the floor of the elevator until they hauled me out of the space. Had I been bleeding?

At the hospital, a dozen or so people stood around me, working away, panic in their eyes. They all looked like they had something to tell me. But when I held my daughter in my arms, staring into that face, their words faded into the background. I stopped listening to what anyone had to tell me. Their talk could wait. Their explanations didn't make sense, anyway.

I vowed from that second onward to never let the pain in my head take me away from Alice's care. She was my world now. Nothing else mattered.

Michael came. I introduced him to his daughter, hoping the love he felt for her would allow him to forgive me for endangering her life in the elevator. But he wouldn't forgive me. His face was filled with anguish over what I had done. I knew right then and there that he would hold on to this moment forever. A wedge had been placed between us that would eventually break our relationship permanently apart.

The doctors came and took Alice away. They told me she needed to go, but I wanted her near. I didn't want her taken away to some room full of newborns so I could rest. I didn't deserve sleep.

The next few days were a blur. I demanded to see Alice, but no one would bring her to me. The doctors kept trying to tell me she was gone, but I couldn't accept that. She was there with me. I held her in my arms. I saw her face. They couldn't tell me otherwise.

People came to visit. I couldn't concentrate on who they were or why they were there. They kept saying how sorry they were. For what? This was a happy occasion. I told them all to stop being sad and to leave after a while.

One of them left behind a plush bunny for Alice. I kept it close by, so she'd have it ready to hold when the doctors brought her back to me.

I held that bunny tight against my chest for days and stroked its back until the doctors sent me home with Michael. At home, I put Alice's bunny in her bassinet, ready for her arrival. As the days went by, I found myself holding Bunny against my chest until I fell asleep. I could never let her go. She was so soft and warm, just like her.

Nothing comforted me like my Bunny. Nothing ever would. She was my Bunny and no one else's.

CHAPTER 43

Now

The ride home is a long one, but I don't mind. Seeing Alice asleep and snuggled up to me is more than I deserve after the hell of a day she's had. She hasn't woken up once, obviously needing her sleep more than anything else.

We cross the George Washington Bridge, finally leaving Manhattan behind. I'll never step another foot inside the city again after today. Michael was wrong. He thought he could take her from me, but Alice is here with me, now and forever.

So many people tried to tell me she didn't exist, that she died before she was born. They were all wrong. How could they have believed it? She is right here with me.

I can feel the softness of her hair as I stroke it. I can feel her warm breath flowing in and out of her body. I can hear her lightly snoring as her heart beats ever so gently. Alice is real. And when we get home, I'll take good care of her.

"How old is your daughter?" the cab driver asks me.

"Just over four years old," I say.

"She's enjoying her sleep, isn't she?"

I nod. "We've had a long day. But we're heading home now for some rest."

"Always a good thing. You're my last fare of the day, then I'm headed home to my own little girl."

"That's wonderful," I reply. "Enjoy your time with her. It's precious."

The driver smiles at me in the mirror and goes back to the task at hand. I stare out the window and think about the future. None of them can bother us now. Michael won't ever see Alice again after today. I won't let him. He can no longer harbor resentment toward me for what happened. It wasn't my fault that Alice almost died in that elevator. If he hadn't placed that stress on me, she would have been okay. He thought he could make it all better with his wealth and control.

We exit the bridge and hit the highway on the long stretch home. I know Alice doesn't enjoy living where we do, but maybe after today, she will come to appreciate the life I've given her. The people around my apartment will welcome us back with open arms. They always have. They always will.

"Mommy? Where are we?" Alice asks, as her eyes half open in a haze of confusion.

I gently lower her head back down and stoke her hair. "Go back to sleep, Bunny. You're safe now. No one can harm you ever again, as long as we stick together. I won't let them."

A LETTER FROM ALEX

I want to say a huge thank you for taking the time to read *The Day I Lost You*. If you enjoyed reading the book and want to keep up to date with all my latest releases, then just sign up using the link below. Your email address will never be shared, and you can unsubscribe at any time.

www.bookouture.com/alex-sinclair

I hope you got a lot out of this book. It was an emotionally challenging story to write, but I loved every minute I spent working on it. If you enjoyed *The Day I Lost You*, I would be very grateful if you took the time to write a review. I'd love to hear your feedback, and your review would help other readers to discover my work.

I also love to hear from my readers. You can get in touch with me on my Facebook page and through Twitter, Goodreads or my website.

Thanks,
Alex Sinclair

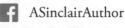 ASinclairAuthor

 ASinclairAuthor

 alexsinclairwrites.com

ACKNOWLEDGEMENTS

A huge thank you to the amazing and hard-working team at Bookouture for making this happen. *The Day I Lost You* underwent many changes from start to finish. It was one of the hardest projects I've worked on to date, but it was well worth the time and effort. It wouldn't have been possible without Commissioning Editor Abigail Fenton. Her knowledge and skills as an editor helped bring this challenging story to light.

A big thank you, as usual, to my wife for her loving support, which got me through every hour of this project. Another big thank you to my young daughter for inspiring me to work hard and push myself to reach new goals.

Thank you to all of the authors at Bookouture, who continue to make me feel like one of the family. I couldn't ask for a better group of people to share my experiences with.

And finally, thank you to anyone who has given my work a chance and spent their valuable time reading this book. Without you, none of this would be possible.

CPSIA information can be obtained
at www.ICGtesting.com
Printed in the USA
FSHW021128121118
53727FS